Frenemy
By
Mark Stephen O'Neal

The Chronicles of Brock Lane

TABLE OF CONTENTS

Chapter 1

The ride home from Chili's restaurant was quick and painless, as the Friday rush hour traffic had dissipated somewhat. The thought of Naomi had eased my tension somewhat and had me looking forward to calling her later on that night. My stepdad's words also resonated in my mind—someone in my inner circle probably leaked information to the kidnappers, and that was how they were able to track us from the airport. But who? I still felt restless and couldn't figure out who might have double-crossed me as I analyzed every friend and associate I'd known in the last five years.

The Uber driver had conversed with me initially but quickly realized I was tired and didn't feel much like socializing. The ride was quiet and peaceful as the radio was tuned into a station that played classic songs from the eighties and nineties. The driver also knew who I was and was dying to ask me for an autograph. However, he only had a few minutes to do so because we reached the Manteno exit.

"Excuse me for asking, Brock," Tony the Uber driver asked, "but aren't you Brock Lane of the St. Louis Trojans?"

"That would be me," I answered.

"Can I have your autograph? I'm a huge Trojan fan and fan of yours, too."

"Sure, no problem."

The driver handed me a small notebook and a pen, and I opened the book and signed it on the third page. I then handed the driver the notebook back and said, "I see I'm not the only autograph in here—that's really dope. How long have you been driving?"

"For a little over two years," Tony answered. "The other two celebrities I had the pleasure of driving around weren't as friendly as you. Thanks."

"No, thank you for making the ride nice and peaceful, Tony," I said.

"My pleasure," Tony said.

Tony pulled up in front of the house moments later, and I got out. I rated Tony five stars and gave him a twenty-dollar tip on the Uber app. My stepfather and Junior were in their respective rooms when I stepped inside, so I tried to make as little noise as possible so that they weren't alerted to my presence because all I wanted to do was sleep once I got settled in. However, Junior came downstairs once I stepped in the kitchen for something to drink.

"What's up, bro?" Junior asked.

"I'm exhausted, man," I answered. "What's Dad doing?"

"He crashed about a half-hour ago. Thanks for getting him home safe."

"You don't have to thank me—I'd put my life on the line for each and every one of you."

Junior paused and asked, "So, what's our next move? I know you're not gonna let them get away with this."

"You're right. I'm not gonna let them get away with this," I answered. "Dad has a friend from the military who's a detective with the CPD, and he's gonna help me track them down."

"I hope so. A million dollars is a lot of money, but they might be bold enough to try us again."

"Time will tell."

"No doubt it will."

"I'll see you in the morning—I'm about to crash, too."

"Okay, talk to you in the morning."

My room was one of the two rooms on the first level of the house, and Nicole, Jasmine, Junior, and Dad each had a room to themselves upstairs. The second room on the first level was primarily used for guests who visited from out of town or friends who spent the night. I changed into a pair of Nike shorts and a wife-beater and plopped on the bed. I then grabbed my cell phone and called Naomi.

"Hi, Brock," she said. "I just walked through the door."

"You want me to give you a minute?" I asked. "I can call you back if you need a wind-down or to get settled in."

"No, don't be silly," she answered. "I'm so happy to hear from you."

"It's good to hear your voice, too. I often wondered if I'd ever see you again."

"Really? Because I was thinking the exact same thing."

"So, why did you leave school?"

"My mother couldn't afford the tuition after she lost her job, so I had to drop out of school before the start of junior year and get a job of my own."

"I was always curious about what happened—I had the biggest crush on you, but you had a boyfriend."

"Devon—things changed between us once I got accepted at Union, if you remember—I guess he couldn't indulge in his sexual escapades as much with me around."

I paused and said, "Yeah, I remember hearing the rumors about him around campus."

She sighed and said, "And as you know, things got worse once he pledged Alpha. We broke up at the end of sophomore year, and things kind of went downhill for me afterwards."

"Once again, I'm really sorry he treated you like that."

"Don't be—everything happened for the best and thank you for being there for me when I needed a shoulder to cry on."

"You're welcome. I'm just happy that I could be some of help to you."

She paused and asked, "Whatever happened to Autumn? I thought you two were going to get married someday."

"Me, too," I answered, "but things change. Let's just say that she saw a better opportunity and took it."

"She left you for another guy, huh?"

"Yes, an investment banker. And can you believe that she called me a few days ago as if nothing ever happened and wanted to pick up where we left off in college?"

"I'm so sorry, Brock. She's got some nerve, and you didn't deserve what she did to you, either."

"It's cool, and I'm over it."

I took a deep breath and said, "Look, I'm just going to put it out there because I don't want to waste your time or mine. I have something to share with you that might change your mind about going out with me."

"Oh, no," she said, "you don't have a venereal disease or something worse, do you?"

"No, nothing remotely close to that," I answered.

"Then what is it?"

"I'm celibate, and I haven't been with anyone since being with my fiancée, Megan."

"Why?"

"Because I'm a born-again Christian, and I'm not having sex again until marriage."

"Wow, I never would've guessed that in a million years—a professional athlete who's celibate. So, tell me, how is that working out for you?"

"I'm just taking it day by day. Some days are harder than others, you know, but I'm good for the most part. I haven't met anyone special—well, no one like you, Naomi."

Megan Gonzales had been a beautiful and curvaceous flight attendant for Southwest Airlines from Orange County, California; and we'd met after my first year in the NBA. She'd flirted with me the entire flight to St. Louis from Los Angeles—giving me special attention over the other passengers on the plane. I'd been visiting my friend and teammate Mike Brown from college after the season was over for a week, and he'd shown me a great time because I'd never experienced the city much except for being in town to play the Lakers or the Clippers.

Megan and I hit it off instantly, and I was ready to marry her after dating for only six months. However, I later learned that she wasn't completely over her ex-boyfriend, so we mutually agreed to break off the engagement. I was disappointed, but I wasn't heartbroken—Autumn's stunt in college prepared me for what was to come. I was grateful for Megan's honesty even though we parted ways, and she eventually went back to her ex. She could've married me, gotten pregnant, and hit me up for child support and alimony; but she didn't. I learned from my canceled engagement to Megan to completely vet the women that I dated from that point on and take no shortcuts, no matter how much I liked any particular one of them.

Most of the women I'd dated since being with Megan lost interest after a certain point—some were honest from the gate and said they couldn't wait until marriage, but the vast majority of them tried to fake the funk for several weeks until they couldn't keep the lie going anymore. The only reason they dated me in the first place was because I played in the NBA, but by the time I figured out that they weren't sincere, I'd already wasted weeks of my time.

I'd also had more than a couple of women try to seduce me—to see if I was really about that life. One woman even called me gay because I refused to have sex with her after she completely disrobed in front of me in her apartment. The last woman I dated was a beautiful sales clerk at a big and tall clothing store I frequented who was always available to talk to me during the day, but I could never reach her at night. She would come up with excuses like she forgot to turn the ringer of her phone back on, or that she was asleep. It turned out that she was heavily into the club scene and was dating multiple men, but she tried to come off as a church girl to get my attention.

"Well, like you, I'm a celibate, born-again Christian who has only been with one guy since Devon," she said, "and I almost got married also. We realized a month before the wedding that neither one of us was ready to walk down the aisle. Needless to say, I've basically compared every guy I've met in the last five years to you, Brock."

"Man, I don't know what to say, Naomi," I said. "I guess the spark I felt at freshman orientation wasn't a figment of my imagination after all."

"No, it definitely wasn't. There was an undeniable spark between us, but, of course, I was with Devon at the time. I'm not the type of girl who cheats on her man."

"I know you're not, and that's why I backed off once you told me you weren't available when we first met. However, seeing you almost every day afterwards was tough for me."

"I know, and I'm sorry. I regret giving Devon chance after chance knowing that he was stepping out on me. If I had it to do all over again, I would've left him for you. I still think about our kiss to this day…"

"I haven't stopped thinking about it, either."

I'd seen Naomi at the quad sitting on one of the benches, crying, one night. It had been almost the end of the second semester of sophomore year at Union, and she had just found out that Devon had cheated on her and gotten another girl pregnant. To make a long story short, I'd tried to comfort her as best I could, and we'd ended up sharing our first and last kiss. I'd felt a spark with her I'd never felt with any woman before or after that, and I'd never seen her again until that Friday in Chili's.

I took a breath and said, "There's no sense in having regrets or dwelling in the past, okay?"

"Okay. So, where do we go from here?"

"I feel like this is our opportunity to really get to know each other—the opportunity that we were denied in college. My only question is: can you handle a long-distance relationship? You know that St. Louis is four hours away."

"Yes, I can. Every other guy I dated since college couldn't handle no sex before marriage, but I feel like you and I are meant to be."

"That's great to hear, because I believe we're meant to be, too. Hey, do you want to go out to dinner tomorrow?"

"I would love nothing more than to go out with you tomorrow, but CeCe is in town for the weekend."

"Oh, yeah? How's CeCe doing?"

"She's fine. She just finished her residency program in Grand Rapids, Michigan."

"That's great—calling her Dr. Daniels is gonna feel kind of weird."

"I know, right?"

"Well, tell her I said hello."

"I most certainly will. Perhaps we can go out Monday after I get off work in the afternoon?"

"Sure, Monday afternoon is fine. Do you like seafood?"

"Yes, I love seafood…"

"This restaurant at Navy Pier has the best seafood in town."

"Great. I'll be home around four on Monday."

"Where do you live?"

"I live in the Sandridge Apartments complex right off 159th and Greenwood. I'll text you the exact address."

"Okay, Naomi, I'll see you tomorrow at five o'clock. And there's one more thing I want to tell you…"

"What is it?"

"You were always my first choice—I wanted you from day one, but I settled for Autumn instead."

"You're giving me goosebumps, Brock—I can't wait to see you."

"I can't wait to see you, too. Bye, Naomi."

"Bye, Brock."

I disconnected the call and smiled. I couldn't believe my sudden good fortune of running into Naomi at the restaurant and couldn't wait for our date on Monday. My endorphin rush was immediately followed by extreme drowsiness, and I was fast asleep once my face hit the pillow.

Chapter 2

The brightness of the sun shone through the blinds and burned my eyes. I hadn't had a good night's sleep in days, as the clock read a quarter past twelve post meridian. My body ached as I slowly rose from my bed and went to the bathroom to relieve my bladder. Junior was watching television in the living room, and my stepdad was gone.

I entered the living room area and asked, "Where's Dad?"

"He had some errands to run," Junior answered.

"I need to borrow his car Monday evening."

"Why?"

"Would you believe that I have a date?"

"Yeah? Anybody I know?"

"Nah, you never met her before. Her name is Naomi, and she went to Union at the same time I did. I saw her at Chili's last night."

"That's great, Brock. I was beginning to worry about you."

"Worry about me?"

"Yeah, you. You haven't been with anybody since Megan—I thought you were gonna join the priesthood or something."

"There's nothing wrong with being selective and waiting for the right person to settle down with. I'm not trying to mess up my life by getting caught up with the wrong girl…especially now, because I'm in the public eye."

"I hear you, and you're absolutely right."

Junior paused briefly and asked, "So, where are you taking her?"

"I'm taking her to Riva Crab House at Navy Pier."

"Sounds like a plan to me…"

"We haven't had a chance to really talk yet, BJ," I said, changing the subject. "Now that you'll be off house arrest in a few weeks, what are your plans for the future?"

"I've had nothing but time to think about this," Junior answered, "and I plan on going to college. Dad pulled some strings and got me into Union this fall."

"That's good, man. Do you know what you're going to major in?"

"Nope, I don't have a clue, but I'll figure it out as I go."

"No doubt."

"I have to get my life on track, man—all of you are doing something with your lives, and I'm tired of being the black sheep of the family."

"Don't be so hard on yourself, okay?"

"I'm just saying…"

"Look, we've all made mistakes, and nobody's perfect. Did you forget that I was in the dope game, too? I could've easily gotten locked up a long time for what I've done…"

"But you didn't. The point is I don't have the luxury of messing up again."

"You'll be all right, BJ. We all have your back."

"Thanks, I appreciate that."

The doorbell rang, and there was a slight knock at the door shortly afterwards. Brock motioned toward the door and answered it.

"What's up, fellas?" Will greeted us as he stepped inside the house.

"It's all good," I said, giving him some dap.

"What's going on, Will?" Junior asked.

"Same ol' stuff," Will answered.

"You get my text?" I asked Will.

"Yeah, I got it," Will answered. "I'm glad your pops is safe. I meant to hit you back, but I got tied up."

"Don't even sweat that," I said.

"What you got going on today?" Will asked.

"Nothing," I answered. "I'm gonna chill right here—just relax and sleep."

"I hear you," Will said. "It's been a rough couple of days."

"What brings you by?" Junior asked.

"I just wanted to check up on my boy," Will answered. "I was in the neighborhood and thought you might've wanted to hang out or something, Brock."

"Nah, I'll catch up with you later," I said. "Maybe I'll come by the shop for a touch-up on Monday."

"That's cool," Will said.

"My sisters will be in town next week for Jaz's graduation party on Friday," I said. "I just got a text from Nikki saying that she'll be here tomorrow."

"Yeah?" Junior asked. "Nobody told me anything."

"It's spur of the moment," I said. "Nikki wants to surprise her."

"So, Jaz doesn't know?" Junior asked.

"Nope," I answered.

"When is Jasmine gonna be in town?" Will asked.

"I don't know," I answered. "She graduated last week."

"Did anybody make it to her graduation?" Will asked.

"Just my dad," I answered. "Nikki was just wrapping up a case, and as you know, I was in Houston for game seven."

"Right," Will said.

"And that's why Nikki wants to throw Jaz a surprise party—because none of us could make her graduation," I said.

"That's what's up," Will said.

"You should slide on through Friday, bro," I suggested to Will.

"Maybe I'll slide through here," Will said. "Well, I'm gonna bounce—later, fellas."

"Wait," I said.

"What's up, fam?" Will asked.

"One of the guys who jacked Pops and I played against us in high school," I answered. "He went to Compton High, but I can't remember his name. I do remember him lighting me up for forty points, though."

"Yeah, I remember that," Will said. "You held your own against him, man."

"Thirty-one points," I said, "but we still lost the game."

"Yeah, we did," Will said. "I gotta go—catch y'all later."

"Later," I said.

Will abruptly left, and Junior was in deep thought and didn't say goodbye to him. I went to the kitchen to grab myself a bottled water and asked, "Are you all right, BJ?"

"Yeah, I'm chill," he answered, "but I wish you wouldn't have invited him to the party, though."

"He's still my friend, BJ."

"That's debatable, bro. Tell me this—why did he come all the way out here just to stay for five minutes? And why did he rush outta here after you told him you remembered one of the guys who robbed you?"

"I don't know..."

"You don't ask enough questions, Brock. Who the hell does he know out here?"

"I don't know that, either—maybe he has relatives in Kankakee or something."

"I'm just saying—nothing adds up with this dude. I was in the game long enough to know when my gut is telling me something."

"What is your gut telling you, BJ?"

"That's he's up to no good, man. You gotta admit that he's being shady."

"Yeah, maybe. He never did respond to my text last night."

"And that's my point. It would've taken him all but five seconds to respond back to you. Our dad gets home safely from being kidnapped by some lowlife scum, and he was too tied up to hit you back?"

"You're right, bro, and I can't defend his actions on this."

"Just keep an eye on him."

"I will."

Chapter 3

The Cubs and the Astros were playing at Wrigley Field on a hot and lazy Saturday afternoon, and Junior and I fell asleep while watching the game. I was still recuperating from the kidnapping ordeal, and my body hadn't fully recovered from a lack of sleep. Junior, on the other hand, usually took a nap around that time, and sleep in the afternoon had become his daily routine since being on house arrest.

My stepdad returned home an hour or so ago from running errands and started cooking a pot of chili. The aroma of the food woke me up, and my stomach was growling. I got up to relieve his bladder once again and greeted him as I motioned to the bathroom.

"Hey, Dad, I didn't hear you come in," I said.

"Yeah, I got back about thirty minutes ago," he said. "I wanted to get a head start on this pot of chili."

"It smells good, and I'm starving," I said.

"It'll be ready soon," Brent said. "I also gave Detective Stanton a call, and he will come by as soon as he can."

"Good. We have to make these guys pay one way or another. As long as they're free, there's nothing stopping them from hitting us again."

"You're absolutely right and make certain that Stanton will catch these guys."

"However, I don't want the press getting wind of this story. They would have a field day if they found out I got robbed by these lowlife thugs."

"I'll let Stanton know how you feel about the situation."

Junior rose up from the sofa and yawned before saying, "I told Brock the same thing last night…we need to track them down before they decide to strike again."

"You aren't tracking anybody down, Junior," Brent said. "We're going to let Stanton do his job."

"What do we know about these guys, Dad?" Junior asked. "Does Stanton even know where to start?"

"We have a license plate number, and one of the guys played basketball for Compton High School in California at the same time that I was in high school," I said. "We can start with that."

"And a cell phone number, even though it's probably a burner cell number," Brent added.

"I'm sure Stanton will know where to start looking for these guys," I said.

I paused and asked, "Can I borrow your car Monday afternoon, Dad?"

"Sure, Brock, I shouldn't be a problem," Brent answered.

"I'll get around to renting a car either Tuesday or Wednesday," I said.

"Take your time, Son," Brent said. "You don't have to rush to rent a car, and you can use mine whenever you need it."

"Thanks, I appreciate it," I said.

The doorbell rang, and Junior got up from the sofa to answer it. Malik then walked in and greeted everyone.

"I'm glad you're safe, Mr. Jones," Malik said.

"Thank you for all of your help, Malik," Brent said. "I wouldn't be standing here if it weren't for you."

"Yeah, thanks again, Malik," Junior added.

"I'm glad I was in a position to help," Malik said.

I gave Malik a hug and said, "I'm glad you're here, bro. You're just in time for some chili."

"Great, because I'm starving," Malik said.

"When are we going to meet Tanya?" I asked.

"Probably never," Malik answered. "We had a huge argument last night, so I left her place and got me a hotel room at the Holiday Inn in Matteson."

"You can stay here as long as you want, Malik," Brent said. "You can sleep in the guest room."

"Thanks, Mr. Jones, but I don't want to impose," Malik said.

"It's no trouble," I said. "It's the least we can do."

"Okay," Malik said.

"What were you arguing with Tanya about?" I asked.

"She was complaining about me coming to town and not spending enough time with her," Malik answered.

"But you just got here a few days ago," I said. "She acts like you all are in a relationship or something."

"I know, right?" Malik asked rhetorically. "I knew I shouldn't have slept with her on the first date."

"You hit that on the first date?" Junior asked.

"Junior," Brent said.

"I'm just sayin', Dad," Junior said.

"It's all right, Mr. Jones," Malik said. "She's mad at me because I wouldn't tell her what was going on with this kidnapping situation. She also thinks there's another woman in the picture…"

"You really need to slow down, Malik," I said. "You just met the girl five minutes ago, and now she's giving you ultimatums? These women got some nerve…"

"Don't just blame the woman, Brock," Brent said. "If you want to roll in the fast lane, be ready to deal with the consequences of driving too fast, Malik."

"You're right, Mr. Jones," Malik said. "I need to practice better judgment."

"You need Jesus," I said.

"You're real funny, Brock," Malik said.

"Who said I was joking?" I said.

"The chili's ready, boys," Brent said.

Each one of us grabbed a bowl out of the cabinet above the kitchen counter and filled our bowls to the rim with my stepfather's secret recipe. The chili contained kidney beans, tomato sauce, spaghetti noodles, ground beef, onions, and secret spices that he wouldn't divulge to us.

"You're gonna have to give me this recipe, Mr. Jones," Malik said. "This chili is delicious."

"Thank you, Malik," Brent said. "I'm glad you like it, but if I give you my recipe, I'll have to kill you."

"Don't feel bad. He told us the same thing," Junior said.

"Maybe I'll share the recipe on my deathbed," Brent said.

"Brock has a date on Monday," Junior said.

"What?" Malik asked. "When did this modern miracle take place?"

"Damn, BJ, you can't hold water," I said.

"I didn't know it was a secret," Junior said sarcastically.

"Anyway, Malik, she's an old friend from college," I said, "and her name is Naomi. I ran into her at Chili's last night."

"That's great, Son," Brent said.

"That's what's up, Brock," Malik said. "The team had a bet to see how long you'd go without being with a woman, and let's just say that I had your back, bro."

"You all were placing secret bets about my love life behind my back?" I asked jokingly. "I'm hurt, Malik."

"I told you everybody thought you wanted to join the priesthood," Junior said.

"Don't let them bother you, Brock," Brent said. "There's nothing wrong with honoring God and sticking to your principles."

"It's okay, Dad," I said. "I can take a joke."

"No, it's not okay, and it's not a joke," Brent said sternly. "There's a reason why I haven't remarried after your mother died."

"Yeah, why?" I said.

"Yeah, what gives?" Junior asked.

"There's profit in our sin," Brent answered.

"You lost me, Dad," Junior said.

"I'm not following you, Mr. Jones," Malik said.

"What I'm saying is the powers that be profit off of us smoking, drinking, fornicating, and committing crimes," Brent said. "As long as we keep doing all those things collectively, society as a whole will continue to get worse."

"Preach, Dad," I said.

"Sexual sin is killing our community the most," Brent said. "Abortion and children born out of wedlock have completely wrecked the Black community, and our desolate state as the result of decades of sexual immorality is judgment."

"Wow, that's deep," Junior said.

"It's the truth," Brent added. "And that's why I support you, Brock. I know it's old-fashioned, but people should really wait until marriage to be intimate with one another."

"I hate to sound morbid, but things aren't going to get better," I said. "Pandora's box is opened, and there's no going back."

"Yeah, people aren't gonna change," Malik said, "and most people aren't waiting until marriage to have sex anymore."

"Well, I'm not going to follow everybody else to hell," I said. "At the same time, I'm not going to browbeat people to do what I'm doing, either. All I can do is present the information, and people can decide for themselves what they want to do."

"That's all you can do, Son," Brent said.

I distinctly remembered getting a Hell message preached to me at least once a month on Sunday in church growing up, and my mother had made sure I knew the Lord before she'd departed from this Earth. The problem in today's church was there was too much preaching about prosperity and not enough preaching about Hell. I believed if more people knew that the consequences of their behavior were a one-way trip to the underworld, they wouldn't do some of the things they did.

"Thanks for the chili, Mr. Jones," Malik said. "That really hit the spot."

"There's plenty more if you want," Brent said.

"No, thank you," Malik said. "I feel like a stuffed pig."

"Yeah, that really did hit the spot, Dad," I said.

"You all are welcome to eat as much as you want," Brent said. "I'll see you guys later...I'm going to my room to take a nap."

"Take care, Mr. Jones," Malik said.

My stepdad retired to his room, and I got up and took everyone's bowl and rinsed them out before putting them in the sink. I made my dishwater before wiping the stove and kitchen counter and said, "I hope I didn't come off too preachy. Sometimes I can't help myself."

"Nah, what you and Dad said needed to be said," Junior said. "It really makes you stop and think about what's going on in the world."

"Yeah, your dad even makes a playa like me wanna change his ways," Malik said.

"Everybody runs out of grace at some point if he or she doesn't change their ways," I said, "and I never want to lose God's favor."

"Amen," Junior said. "Enough with church, fellas...what's up for later?"

"Brian Dawson and Paul Carter of the Chicago Bulls are throwing a party in the Gold Coast area tonight," Malik answered. "Are you still down, Brock?"

"I don't know," I answered. "I'll see how I'm feeling a little later."

"Damn, I wish I could go," Junior said. "You should hang out with Malik, Brock."

"Come on, bro, it'll be fun," Malik added. "You need to relax and keep your mind off what just happened. Besides, you need to see what else is out here before you propose to Naomi."

"You-are-hilarious, Malik," I said sarcastically. "I don't need to see what else is out here because I already know that there's nothing but trouble in these streets."

"Suit yourself, Brock," Malik said. "I'll be back in a little bit...I'm gonna check out of the hotel and get my suitcase."

"Okay, cool," I said. "I'll let you know if I'm going or not when you come back."

"Solid," Malik said. "Later."

Malik let himself out as I finished washing the dishes.

"Malik's a true friend, Brock," Junior said. "You should hang out with him tonight and forget about Will. You can go to my barber in Hazelcrest instead of going to the city on Monday."

"Yeah, I'm going to hang out with him tonight," I said.

"Good. Malik's right about one thing..."

"What's that?"

"You should leave your options open. Who knows? You might meet someone who's gonna give your girlfriend some competition."

"I like to keep things simple...my life isn't the next episode of *The Bachelor*."

"I hear you, bro."

"I'm gonna take a shower."

"All right, I'll be in my usual spot on the couch."

Chapter 4

Will parked his BMW X5 truck in front of Terrence and Russell's apartment right off Grant Street and 11th Ave in Gary, Indiana. He crashed over there yesterday after they split up the stolen cash.

Will had met Terrence senior year, during a tournament game in Compton, California, after Terrence's team soundly beat his team and Terrence had scored forty points on them. Will had had to be creative in thinking of a way to break curfew and go to a house party that Terrence had mentioned, and they'd been thick as thieves ever since then.

"I see you found the spot," Terrence said. "How did you slip past your coach?"

"Can't nothing or nobody hold me for too long," Will answered.

"Let's go holla at some of these girls, man," Terrence said.

They stepped inside of the house as the DJ was playing a rap song that Will didn't recognize. He turned toward Terrence and asked, "Who's that rapping on this song?"

"He's an underground rapper named A$AP Rocky," Terrence answered. "You never heard of him?"

"Nah, they don't play this type of music in Chicago. This song is dope as hell."

"Yeah, this song is my joint, Will."

Terrence glanced to his left and saw three guys with red bandannas on their heads mean-mugging them. Terrence turned and whispered in Will's ear, "Don't look up—I might have to bust some heads up in here. This fool I beat down for hitting my sister is staring at us."

"Don't worry, ain't nothing gonna pop off right here," Will said, revealing to Terrence that he had a gun tucked on his waist.

"How you get a gun out here?"

"Your teammate Brian told me where I could cop one cheap. I'mma dump it before we catch the plane back home."

"You a D-boy?"

"I was before me and my man Brock got pinched last summer."

"Word. How come your man didn't kick it to this party, fam?"

"He's different, man. He acts like he ain't down no more after we got out of jail."

"How long were y'all locked up?"

"Most of the summer…about two months. His dad has some connections and got us probation."

"That's what's up."

The three guys who were giving Will and Terrence the evil eye approached them while they were standing near the DJ on the turntables. Will never lost eye contact with the lead thug.

"What's up now, homeboy?" the lead thug asked.

"You tell me, DeShaun," Terrence answered. "You put your hands on my sister, and I settled it. There's nothing else to talk about."

"Nah, my man, you ain't settled a damn thing," DeShaun said. "Your sister cheated on me…did she tell you that?"

"Whatever, man," Terrence said. "That doesn't give you the right to punch her in the face—"

"You heard my man," Will interjected, raising his shirt to reveal his concealed gun. "The beef is settled, so I suggest you step off and move on."

"And who the hell are you?" the second thug asked.

"Don't worry about who I am," Will answered. "You keep running your damn mouth, you gonna catch a bad break."

"Come on, fellas, let's bounce," DeShaun said. "This ain't over, Terrence."

"I'm right here, homeboy," Terrence said.

The three Piru Bloods left the party, and Terrence said, "Thanks for having my back, Will."

"I got you, fam," Will said.

"We better get the hell outta before they come back and spray the joint," Terrence urged. "DeShaun got an AK-47 that he's quick to let loose."

"All right," Will said. "Let's hit this weed I got somewhere."

"Cool, I got a spot we can go to," Terrence said.

Will continued to sit in his truck and briefly reflect on the past while he finished puffing on his blunt. He was also upset about the fact that Brock recognized Terrence as one of the kidnappers. Moments later, he stepped onto the porch of Terrence and Russell's house that they rented and went inside as the front door was opened.

"What's up, fam?" Terrence asked. "Russ stepped out for a minute."

"We got a problem," Will answered.

"What is it?"

"Brock remembers who you are. He doesn't remember your name, though."

"Yeah?"

"I'm afraid so."

"I guess I left a lasting impression on him."

"Time isn't on our side, so we have to figure out a way to hit them quick and leave the country for good."

"Russ will be back soon, so we can hammer out a game plan then."

"They're throwing a surprise party for Brock's little sister Jasmine on Friday. She just graduated from college."

"You think Malik will be there?"

"I don't know…I'll think of a smooth way to ask Brock if he'll be there."

"There's no sense in hitting them up again if he isn't in town for the party. There's probably not gonna be nobody else with some real money there."

"Nah, there will be one more person there with some loot."

"Who, Brock?"

"Not Brock…his sister Nikki. She's a partner at the biggest law firm in D.C."

"Cool…I got a plan that should work. It will give us enough money to leave the country for good."

"What's the plan?"

"I'll break it down when Russ comes back."

"Save that thought, fam. I gotta get back to the shop."

"All right, let's meet up tomorrow at your crib then."

"Yeah, that's cool…y'all can slide on through at about noon. Later."

"Later, fam."

Chapter 5

Naomi was on her way to Cecilia's house to pick her up because they were going out to dinner and a movie afterwards. She had gotten her car out the shop and spent almost a grand getting new brakes and rotors, and this bill nearly depleted her savings.

Cecilia Daniels' family lived in Hyde Park, which was a neighborhood right off the lakefront and was about five miles from downtown Chicago. The plan was to eat dinner at any restaurant at Block 37 on Washington and State Street and see the movie *Black Panther*. She finished up her residency program at Spectrum Health in Grand Rapids, Michigan, and she had come home for Mother's Day weekend to hang out with the family and Naomi.

Naomi luckily found a parking space in front of Cecilia's parents' spacious home on Woodlawn Avenue. She parked her car and walked toward the house. Cecilia greeted her on the front porch once she saw Naomi walking up the steps.

"Hey girl," Cecilia said, giving Naomi a warm embrace.

"It's so good to see you, CeCe," Naomi said. "How does it feel to be done with your program?"

"It feels great, but there's no rest for the weary."

"Are you come back to Chicago?"

"Probably not right away. I don't know where I'll end up, though. I'm going to work my first several years in a distressed area of the country to alleviate a good portion of my student loan debt."

"That sounds like a plan. Are you ready to go?"

"Yes, and I'm starving."

"Where do you want to eat? We don't have to dine at Block 37—there's plenty of other restaurants in the area to choose from."

"We don't have to go anywhere fancy. What about Ronny's Steakhouse?"

"That's fine with me because I'm on a budget anyway. The brakes on my car really set me back a few pennies."

"Don't worry about it, Nae Nae. Dinner's on me. Money isn't a problem for me yet—I don't start paying back my enormous student loan debt for another six months."

"Nah, I'm good, CeCe. Dinner and a movie aren't gonna break me."

"Okay, girl."

They hopped in Naomi's car and headed toward Lakeshore Drive. Cecilia was a caramel-complected young woman who was just as beautiful as Naomi, but she had more of an Afrocentric style with the dreadlocks and African jewelry, whereas Naomi looked more like a fashion model with the designer purse and matching Gucci pumps.

"So, how long are you staying in town?" Naomi asked.

"I go back on Wednesday," Cecilia answered.

"What is there to do in Grand Rapids?"

"Not a whole lot. The Gerald Ford Museum is there, and we have a zoo if you're into that kind of stuff. I'm basically consumed with work and studies anyway."

"I hear you."

Naomi paused and said, "I have a date on Monday, and you'll never guess who I'm going out with."

"Yeah?" Cecilia asked. "And who is this lucky man?"

"Brock..."

"Brock Lane? You're lying..."

"No, CeCe, I'm serious. He came to Chili's last night out the blue, and we exchanged numbers."

"He really asked you out, huh? Wow, Nae Nae, that's great—running into Brock like that—it is a dream come true for you."

"Yeah, I'm still floating on cloud nine—he called me the same night and said I was always his first choice and that he settled for Autumn because he couldn't have me."

"Sounds romantic..."

"I know, right? I waited so long for someone special to come into my life, and now he's here."

"I can't wait to hear all of the details after your date on Monday."

"There's someone special out here for you, too," Naomi said sincerely. "You're way too fine to be still be single."

"Thank you for your concern, but I'll be okay," Cecilia said. "There is someone at work who likes me a lot, but I'm not feeling him like that."

"Really? What's wrong with him?"

"He's just not my type—I've never dated outside my race before, and there's just not a whole lot of Black men to choose from in Grand Rapids."

"What does the guy look like?"

"His name is Aryan, and he's from India or Pakistan I believe. He's cute, but he's shorter than me."

"How much shorter?"

"I don't know—he's five-seven or five-eight maybe…"

"You're gonna meet lots of guys who are shorter than you, CeCe—you're six feet tall. Maybe you should relax your standards a little bit."

"Why should I settle for someone who I'm not attracted to? You didn't."

"You're right—touché. I just want to see you happy."

"Thanks, I appreciate it."

Cecilia sighed and said, "Mr. Brock Lane—are you sure you're built for his type of lifestyle?"

"What are you saying exactly?"

"Brock's on the road a great deal during the season, and let's just say that there are endless groupies vying for his attention."

"He's not like that, CeCe…"

"Like what, Nae? He's a man, so don't be naive about the situation."

"He's a born-again Christian, and he's been celibate like me for the past couple of years."

"And you believe him?"

"Yeah, why wouldn't I believe him?"

"Because it sounds too good to be true. There's no such thing as a celibate pro athlete."

"Damn, why are you hating?"

"I'm not hating on you—I'm just looking out for you like a true friend is supposed to do. He's got you wide open."

"I'm gonna take things slow, CeCe."

"You better—you don't want to end up being a baby's mama."

"Whatever."

They were in downtown Chicago before they knew it and at the diner several minutes after that, even though traffic was slightly heavy on an early Saturday evening. Naomi parked in a nearby garage, and they walked a block or so to the diner. The line was relative short, and they ordered their choice of the buffet-style food and sat in a booth near the window.

"I haven't been here in a long time," Cecilia said. "I love the food."

"Me, too," Naomi said. "I come here sometimes after class."

"One more semester, huh?"

"Yep, six more hours, and I'm done."

"Are you going to finish up in the summer or fall?"

"I'm gonna finish up in summer school so that I can graduate in August."

"Do you have a job lined up after graduation?"

"I have a few prospects, but I want to take the CPA exam first before I start applying for those jobs. I've been studying as much as can whenever I have some free time because I've taken all of the classes within my major."

"That makes perfect sense."

Cecilia paused and said, "Do you plan on staying in Chicago?"

"I don't know," Naomi answered. "I haven't given it much thought. Who knows? I might relocate to St. Louis if Brock and I become serious."

"That is definitely something to consider."

Naomi took a sip of her soda and looked toward the entrance. A few seconds later, June from the breakfast diner where she worked walked in. He had his CTA uniform on and looked like he'd just finished his shift. Cecilia stared at him in disgust and seemed as if she knew him also.

"What's wrong with you, CeCe?" Naomi asked.

"I know that guy," Cecilia answered.

"So do I," Naomi said. "He comes by the diner I work at all the time. He's such a sweet guy—he flirts with me all the time, but he's not my type."

"He's a jerk..."

"CeCe..."

June spotted them at their table and stepped out of line to greet them. He made eye contact with Naomi first.

"Hey, Naomi," June said before looking at Cecilia. "Cecilia? Is that you?"

"Hi, June," Naomi said. "You know my best friend?"

"June Summers," Cecilia said, "you've got some nerve..."

"Wait, Cecilia, I can explain," June said.

"Explain what, June?" Cecilia asked. "There's nothing to explain. Come on, Nae Nae, I'm ready to go!"

"Wait, Cecilia, it's not what you think it is," June pleaded. "Just hear me out first, and if you still want to leave, I won't try to stop you."

"What do you want?" Cecilia asked angrily.

"The night we met was the most incredible night I ever had," June said solemnly. "I'm sorry I never called you again, baby. There isn't a day that goes by that I don't think about you..."

"I don't accept or buy your apology, June," Cecilia said. "You couldn't find the time to call me in five years?"

"Wait, you two met at Union?" Naomi asked.

"No, we met at a frat party in Bloomington," Cecilia answered. "June went to Illinois State—we had a one-night stand, and he never called me again after that."

"Is that true, June?" Naomi asked. "You dogged out my girl?"

"No, Naomi, it wasn't even like that," June answered.

"None of this makes any sense," Naomi said.

"Please, just let me finish," June said.

"You have five seconds," Cecilia said.

"I fell in love with you after the night we had," June said. "I had every intention of calling you that same day to make sure you got back to campus safely, but someone stole my cell phone out of my car that morning..."

"You expect me to believe that?" Cecilia said.

"I swear I'm telling the truth, baby," June said. "I thought I'd never see you again, and here you are. I love you, Cecilia..."

"Come on, CeCe," Naomi said, "look at him. You can't see that he's telling the truth?"

"All of my information was on that phone," June continued. "My phone numbers, pictures, podcasts and even some of my notes from class—my whole life was practically on that phone. And to add insult to injury, the thief broke out my driver side window to steal my phone. It took me a month to get my window fixed and be able to afford another phone, and by then, the semester was over."

"I need time to process all of this," Cecilia said. "I called you repeatedly for days after you hung up on me and blocked my number, and then your number was disconnected permanently. You broke my heart..."

"I didn't hang up on you or block your number, and I didn't mean to break your heart," June affirmed. "I had to report that my phone was stolen, and that's why my number was disconnected. I promise I will never hurt you again."

"I'll give you two some time to work this out," Naomi said. "I'll call you later on tonight, CeCe, okay?"

"Okay," Cecilia said, wiping the tears from her eyes.

"Don't worry, Naomi," June said, "I'll get her home safe. She's in good hands."

"I know," Naomi said. "I'll see you both later."

"Bye, Nae Nae," Cecilia said. "I love you."

"I love you, too," Naomi said as she left the two of them sitting at the booth by the window and exited the diner.

Chapter 6

Malik and I were on our way to the Saturday evening bash hosted by our NBA rivals Brian Dawson and Paul Carter. The dynamic duo of the Chicago Bulls gave our team all that we could handle as we split the season series two games to two. Brian Dawson was the front runner for the league MVP and the best center in the eastern conference, and Paul Carter was one of best guards and two-way players in the league at six foot five.

Malik had befriended the two of them at last year's all-star game and would hang out with them on occasion, and I was just along for the ride because I didn't know either of them outside of playing against one another. In fact, Malik had friends on a good portion of the teams in the league, but I didn't socialize with anyone other than our teammates off the court. I was a loner who shunned the spotlight most of the time and rarely frequented parties or clubs, but Malik was the exact opposite.

"This is gonna be the party of the summer, Brock," Malik said. "A lot of A-list people were invited."

"That's cool," I said.

"You don't sound too excited."

"You know it's not my scene, bro."

"You need to liven up a little bit."

"I'm at a different place in my life, Malik. No disrespect, but I could care less about meeting any celebrities, man."

"You're a celebrity, Brock…"

"No, I'm not—I play basketball, and I'm good at it—nothing more, nothing less."

"I love your humility, homie, but you're a celebrity whether you like it or not."

We arrived downtown at a little before dusk, and traffic was at a standstill at the Dan Ryan/Kennedy split. Malik looked at me and said, "I should get off at 22nd Street, shouldn't I?"

"Yeah," I answered, "but take North I-55 to Lakeshore Drive and exit at North Avenue."

"Okay."

The club was located on the Wells Street strip in between Division Street and North Avenue. There were a slew of nightclubs and restaurants on this half-mile stretch, and the spot was jumping on Friday and Saturday nights no matter what time of the year it was. If you were man or woman under the age of thirty, this was the place to be.

We arrived at the club about twenty minutes later, and Malik valeted the car before we went inside the club. The bass of the music was thumping, and the dance floor was packed as we tried to make our way to VIP.

"You wanna dance, Brock?" this beautiful young lady asked me before we could get to our spot.

"Sure, you lead the way," I answered. "I'll catch up with you in a minute, Malik."

"Handle your business, my brother," Malik said.

I followed the young lady to the dance floor, and she had a tongue ring and smelled like Gucci Bamboo and cigarettes. We danced for a good while before I asked her, "Do you want something to drink, pretty lady?"

"Yes, please," she answered.

"What's your name?" I asked.

"Monique," she answered.

"Nice to meet you, Monique," I said.

"Likewise," she said.

"What are you drinking?" I asked.

"Sex on the Beach," she answered seductively.

We walked over to the bar, and I ordered our drinks. I grabbed my virgin cranberry juice and handed Monique her cocktail before saying, "You're welcome to join us in VIP if you want."

"I'd love to," she said. "Can I bring my two friends?"

"Sure. Where are they?" I asked.

"At the table over there," she said, pointing to a booth in the corner of the club.

We walked toward her friends' table as the club became even more packed. Monique had a stout and shapely figure—she was about five foot three or four; and she had a noticeably small waist, plump derriere, wide hips, and thick thighs. Her skin was olive brown, and she appeared to be of both African American and Asian descent. Her friends were just as beautiful—one young lady was an African American, model-like beauty, and the other beauty was a Caucasian young woman with long and dark brunette hair and a slim but shapely figure. My first impression of them was that they all were undeniably hot, but they were agents of chaos.

I got approached by women quite frequently, and that night was simply par for the course. However, my selection process was very thorough because I was always going to approach every woman I met with much scrutiny.

"This is Tameka," Monique said, "and this is Ashley."

"Nice to meet you both," I said. "Follow me, ladies."

I led them to the VIP section of the club, and Malik and Paul were in there with two other beautiful young ladies. I introduced my new friends to the group, and Paul followed suit. Each of the young ladies said hello to each other, and I said, "Nice to meet you all."

"Nice to meet you too, Brock," Brenda said.

"Nice to meet you," Vicki said, grabbing my hand and smiling at me. "I'm sorry about your team losing to Houston. I'm a huge fan."

"Thank you," I said. "We'll see what happens next season."

"Yeah, we'll surely bring the trophy home next season," Malik added. "St. Louis deserves a championship, and we're gonna give them one."

"I love your confidence, homeboy," Paul said. "You're gonna have to go through us to get there."

"How have you been, Paul?" I interjected, giving him some dap.

"I've been good," Paul answered. "Thanks for coming to my party."

"No problem, bro," I said. "Where's Brian?"

"He's around here somewhere," Paul answered.

"Do you come here often whenever you're in town?" Monique asked me.

"No, I don't," I answered. "I usually chill out with my family whenever I'm back in town."

"Aw, that's no fun," Monique said. "You should get out more often because you're really a great dancer."

"Thank you, Monique," I said.

"You're welcome," Monique said.

Flattery feels great—especially when it comes from a beautiful woman—but I always proceeded with caution whenever a woman I didn't know complimented me. Many brothers in my position have fallen prey to women who had nothing but nefarious intentions. However, I continued to give my full attention to Monique in spite of that fact and didn't converse with the other women or Malik and Paul.

"So, you kick it just about every weekend, huh?" I asked.

"Yeah, every chance I get, honey," she said. "You only live once, and I'm gonna live life to the fullest while I'm still young."

"How old are you?"

"I'm twenty-two."

"Yeah, you and me both still got a lot of living to do, sweetheart. Are you in college?"

"Yes—I'll be in my fifth year at Loyola in the fall—I've got one more year, and I'll be done with undergrad."

"That's what's up. What are you majoring in?"

"I'm a political science major. I'm thinking about law school next year, but I'm not sure—I already have well over one hundred thousand dollars in student loans."

"A lawyer, huh? Law's a great field. I majored in communications while I was in school, and I may go into broadcasting once I retire from playing."

"You should, because you're very photogenic."

"And you're very photogenic as well."

"Thank you, Brock."

"You're very welcome."

"Enough about me. So, Brock, tell me a little about yourself."

"There's really not much to tell. What you see is what you get."

"I highly doubt that. You seem like a complicated man."

"I'm not that complicated. I like to keep life simple—I put God first, my family second, and basketball third."

"God, family, and basketball, huh? Yeah, I'll say that's pretty straightforward."

She paused and asked, "Do you have a girlfriend?"

"Yes, as a matter of fact, I do have someone very special in my life."

"How serious are you about your girlfriend, huh?" she said, grabbing my hand. "You could have a little fun on the side to spice up your relationship—you feel me?"

"You've got me all wrong, Monique," I answered, pulling my hand away. "I'm not that kind of guy, and I thought we were just trying to get to know each other and enjoy each other's company."

"My bad," she said, "I thought you'd be down for whatever."

"I'm sorry, Monique," I said. "I didn't mean to give you the wrong impression."

Monique gave me a reptilian-like glare and turned her attention to the rest of the group, and she didn't acknowledge my apology. She was obviously turned off by me rejecting her aggressive advances, but I really didn't care. I knew at that point she deemed me as a colossal waste of her time and was on the hunt for another baller. My impression of her after that was if she put more energy into school than chasing wealthy men, she'd be finished with undergrad and be in law school instead of five years of undergrad. She was smart but wasn't focused.

It wouldn't surprise me at all if Malik or Paul ended up hooking up with her that night. The club wasn't my scene anymore, and I wasn't being true to myself by trying to impress some random woman just because that was what superstar athletes were supposed do.

I then got up after a few minutes of being shunned by Monique and tried to make my way to the entrance of the club before I felt a hand on my shoulder. I turned around and saw that it was Brian Dawson.

"What's up, Brock?" he asked. "Leaving already?"

"Hey, Brian," I greeted him. "Nah, I'm gonna get some air."

"Is everything okay?"

"Yeah—everything's cool. I'll be back in a few minutes."

"Oh, okay."

I left the club and strolled down Wells Street in the direction of North Avenue. The summer's night breeze blew some cool air off of the lake, and there was much commotion as traffic on Wells Street was at a standstill. There was a Walgreens on the northeast corner of Wells and North, so I went inside to get a pack of gum.

I was still mad at myself for letting Monique get under my skin after she ignored me. I guess her disingenuousness took me back to a place in my life when I wasn't popular or successful—like the time when I was a tall and lanky kid in the ninth grade who couldn't get any play from the girls at school, and I'd be the invisible guy holding up the wall at a typical high school dance. It wasn't until I made the starting lineup on the varsity basketball team sophomore year that girls started taking notice.

I subsequently went to the aisle where the gum and candy were and grabbed a pack of Mentos gum, paid the cashier, and left. I took my time heading back to the club, and I even signed a few autographs along the way.

Chapter 7

There was a knock at the door after the doorbell rang, and Junior rushed out the bathroom to answer it. Brent was upstairs in his room and didn't respond to the doorbell.

"May I help you?" Junior asked as he opened the door.

"I'm here to see Brent Jones," the middle-aged Caucasian man answered.

"And who are you?" Junior asked with a suspicious tone in his voice.

"I'm Blaine Stanton," he answered, "a friend of your dad's."

"Oh, okay," Junior said. "I'll get him for you."

"Thank you."

Junior went upstairs to get his father. His natural distrust of cops reared its ugly head in the form of a rude greeting at the front door, and he was unapologetic for it.

"Hey, Dad, that cop you called for Brock's case is here," Junior said.

"Okay, Son," Brent said. "Tell him I'll be down in a minute."

Junior went back downstairs and let Stanton know that his dad would be downstairs shortly. He then resumed watching television and didn't say another word. He would subsequently turn off the television and go upstairs to his room once Brent came downstairs.

"Good to see you, old friend," Brent said, shaking Stanton's hand. "Thank you for coming by on such short notice."

"No problem," Stanton said. "Anything for you, brother."

"Did Junior offer you something to drink?"

"No, he didn't. I'll have some water if you don't mind."

"Sure, no problem."

Brent grabbed a bottled water out the refrigerator and handed it to Stanton. Stanton sighed and asked, "So, what happened, Brent?"

"I'm still trying to wrap my mind around it," Brent answered. "Basically, these punks kidnapped me to get money out of Brock and succeeded in doing so."

"Why didn't Brock call the police?"

"The kidnappers lied and said a dirty cop contracted them for the job, and Brock didn't want to risk my life or his and complied with their demands. Plus, Brock didn't want the press all over this story."

"I see. So, here's what I need for you to do—tell me as much as you can about what happened from start to finish."

Brent gave Stanton the spill from the time he picked Brock up from the Peotone Airport to the final meeting in the parking lot of the baseball diamond off East 126th Street. He gave Brent specific details about being bound to a bedpost and his conversations with both guys.

"Did you get their license plate number?" Stanton asked.

"Yes, the plate read *MR GRIM*," Brent answered.

"Do you know anything else about them that may help with the investigation?"

"And one of the guys was a superstar athlete at Compton High in California around the same time Brock was in high school. He played both football and basketball, and he was all-state in both sports."

"When did Brock graduate high school?"

"He graduated in 2011."

"Okay, that should be enough to get me started, and I'll file a police report on your behalf and be in touch with an update in a couple of days."

"Will you be able to prevent this story from being leaked to the press?"

"I don't know, Brent. I'll try my best to keep it quiet, but the amount of the ransom will raise eyebrows."

"Okay, just do what you can and thanks, Blaine. If I think of anything else, I'll call you."

"Okay."

Brent shook Stanton's hand and walked him to the door. Stanton turned around and said, "I promise you we will catch these guys, Brent."

"I have no doubt that you will. See you in a few days."

"Take care."

Brent looked on from the front porch as Stanton pulled off, and he came back inside and summoned Junior to the living room a minute or so later.

"What's your problem, son?" Brent asked.

"Nothing, Dad," Junior answered. "What are you talking about?"

"You know what I'm talking about. Why didn't you offer Detective Stanton something to drink?"

"Dad, you're trippin'. What did he say to you?"

"He didn't have to say anything. All I know is I taught you better than that."

"Sorry, Dad. It won't happen again."

"You know, Son, you're never going to get anyway in life with that temper of yours. Nobody forced you to sell drugs and get busted, so take ownership for what you've done and adjust your attitude."

"Yes, sir…"

"I'm going back upstairs…finish up those dishes in the sink."

"Okay."

Chapter 8

I went back in the club after a half-hour and took a seat at the bar. There was no way in hell that I was going back to VIP to deal with the phoniness of those superficial women and the bravado of my comrades.

"What you drinking, Brock?" the bartender asked.

"Let me have another cranberry juice," I answered.

"Coming right up."

The bartender placed my drink in front of me moments later, and it was then that I noticed my ex-girlfriend from high school sitting two seats down from me. She smiled once we made eye contact with each other, and as fate would have it, the seat next to me was vacant. This night couldn't get any worse, I thought.

"Mister Brock Lane," Michelle greeted me.

"Miss Michelle Jackson," I greeted her back. "It's still Miss Jackson, right?"

"Yes, it is. How have you been?"

"I can't complain too much. I've been blessed."

"You most definitely have, and I'm definitely one of your biggest fans, Brock."

I ignored her comment, and I took a sip of my cranberry juice and asked, "So, what have you been up to?"

"I just finished law school, and I just passed the bar exam," she answered. "I already got an offer to work at this firm downtown where I did my summer internship last year."

"That's great, Michelle. Congratulations."

"Thank you."

"What are you drinking?"

"Patron and cranberry."

"I got you."

I ordered her another round and asked, "What brings you here on a Saturday night?"

"I don't live too far from here," she answered. "I stay in the apartment complex right off Wells and Chicago Avenue. I'm supposed to be meeting some of my colleagues from work for drinks tonight."

"Sounds good."

"And you?"

"Paul Carter and Brian Dawson are throwing a party here in the VIP room."

"Why aren't you in there?"

"Not my scene, Michelle—gold-digging thots and macho ballplayers trying to get laid ain't my cup of tea."

"Funny, I thought all of you professional athletes craved that type of attention."

"Not all of us…"

"That's good to know. Can you do me a favor?"

"Sure, what is it?"

"I need to go to the ladies room pronto. Can you hold my seat?"

"Yeah, go ahead."

"Thanks, Brock."

"No problem."

Michelle quickly made her way to the bathroom as if her bladder was about to explode, and I chuckled to myself and shook my head. Michelle was surprisingly a breath of fresh air, and she seemingly brightened my dismal night as my urge to ditch the club and catch an Uber home disappeared. She was still very attractive, but her aura was totally different. She seemed to be very mature and polished—a far cry from the stuck-up cheerleader I'd once known in high school. The five foot eight inch, chocolate beauty was now a grown woman.

"I'm back," she said. "Did you miss me?"

"Ah, I guess so," I said jokingly. "You aiight."

"Boy, you're so silly."

She paused for a second and grabbed my hand before saying, "Seriously, there's something I want to say to you, Brock."

"What?" I asked.

"I'm sorry for the way I treated you back in high school. You didn't deserve what I did to you…"

"You mean what you did with Will?"

She paused again and sighed before she answered, "Yes, I slept with Will one time, and it was one of the worst mistakes of my life. I hope you can find it in your heart to forgive me."

"I forgave you a long time ago, and our breakup wasn't totally your fault, Michelle. I completely shut you out once my mom died, and for that I'm very sorry."

"I wanted to be there for you, but I didn't know how to comfort you…"

"It's okay—there's no need to beat yourself up about this."

"So, Will told you about us?"

"Not exactly. My brother told me about what went down because he saw you two in the Walgreens parking lot off 87th Street one day right before graduation…"

"You confronted him about it, and he came clean, huh?"

"Yeah, but he would've taken it to the grave if I never said anything."

"And you're still friends with him?"

"Yeah, you know the saying—keep your friends close and your enemies closer."

"How close are you to him?"

"We're not as close as we once were, but I still keep up with him whenever I'm in town. I was the one who helped him get his barbershop up and running."

"Really?"

"Yes, I gave him the startup money to get it off the ground."

"I see…"

"What, you know something?"

"I heard from a reliable source that he launders dope money out of that barbershop," she leaned over and whispered in my ear. "I didn't know you helped him open it up."

"How do you know this?" I asked, whispering back in her ear.

"My friend Lolita messes around with Will off and on, and she was the one who told me."

"Damn, this is bad—really bad."

"I know."

"If word ever gets out that I funded his little enterprise, my contract could be null and void."

"You should distance yourself from him as soon as possible, Brock. A scandal is the last thing you need."

"What else do you know about him?"

"I've only seen Will a couple of times since high school—most notably when Lolita brought him to my twenty-fifth birthday party earlier this year. I also found out that he runs with two guys from Compton, California."

"Word? What are their names?"

"One of the guys is named Russell, and he's a slim, dark-skinned guy with light brown eyes."

"And the other guy?"

"He's a tall, light-skinned guy with a muscular body like a football player. His name is Terrence."

"Terrence? Do you know his last name?"

"No, I don't know either one of their last names."

"Oh, okay."

Things clicked for me when she told me Will ran with two guys from Compton—I knew at that very moment Will was the one who set me up. Michelle described my stepfather's captors to a T, and Will was the one and only person who could've known when I was going to be at the airport. He must have studied my routine to the most intricate detail, and my predictability proved to be my downfall. However, I was going to need concrete proof to bring Will's crew down.

I also knew deep down that all the evidence pointed directly at Will, even though his involvement was too painful to admit to myself. His ultimate act of betrayal was unfathomable to me, and I tried to explore every other possibility before drawing that conclusion.

Michelle took a breath and said, "You know, our chance encounter was much easier than I envisioned it being. I said to myself that if I ever saw you again, I'd come clean about what happened back then…"

And I want to come clean about what I did, too."

40

"I already know about you and Joanne Rogers hooking up after we broke up. She always had a thing for you."

"But she was your best friend…"

"No, she wasn't—and she couldn't wait to let me know that you confided in her, and that one thing led to another."

"Yeah, that was a big mistake."

"Well, what's done is done," she said. "We were still kids back then, but we're all grown up now."

"Yes, here's to being grownups," I said as we toasted our glasses.

She took a deeper breath and said, "I hope we can still be friends, Brock."

"I don't see any harm in that," I said.

"Great, and if you ever need an attorney, here's my card."

"Thank you, I'll keep that in mind."

"Well, I see my friends over there near the entrance. Take care of yourself."

"You, too, Michelle."

We stood up and gave each other a warm embrace, and she kissed me on the cheek before she walked toward the entrance to greet her friends. I glanced over her business card before placing it in my pocket, and I sat back down at the bar to finish my drink.

No good deed goes unpunished—I knew the Lord would reveal who was responsible for the kidnapping and robbery in due time after I prayed about it. Will was possessed with the dangerous spirit of envy that he ever so adeptly masked—even after I funded his barbershop—and my blind trust in him nearly cost me my life as well as my stepdad's life. However, I couldn't let my anger toward him cloud my judgment, and if I was going to take Will and his crew down, I had to keep a clear and level head in order to stay two steps ahead on the chess board.

I observed Monique and Paul dancing a few feet away from where I was sitting and didn't notice Malik standing behind me. He tapped me on the shoulder and asked, "Where have you been? Everybody's asking about you."

"Hey, bro, I'm just chillin' right here," I answered.

"You're not coming back to VIP?"

"Nah, man, I'm gonna stay here at the bar."

"What's wrong, Brock? Is it Monique?"

"I'm not thinking about Monique or any of those other girls up there. Everything's okay, Malik."

"I thought Monique was really feelin' you, though."

"She was until I let know in no uncertain terms that I wasn't trying to get caught in her web. Paul can have her, but he'd better wrap it up."

"Why do you say that?"

"Something tells me that she's looking for a sponsor to pay off her student loans or something to that effect. She's way too thirsty for me."

"I hear you."

There was brief silence, and I said, "I think I'm gonna bounce, bro. I'll catch an Uber, so don't worry about me."

"You sure? Because I can wrap things up here, and we can leave out together."

"Nah, man, don't let me rain on your parade. My path is my path—I don't expect you or anyone else to live the way I live."

"All right then, old man."

"Here, take my key. BJ can let me in."

"Okay, see you later, Brock."

"Later."

Malik walked toward the back of the club where a group of women were standing along with Brian Dawson and a couple of other guys from the Bulls and a guy I recognized from the Bears, and I finished my glass of cranberry juice before tipping the bartender. I then proceeded to request a ride on the Uber app and stepped outside to meet the driver, who was a minute away. I had a forty-five minute to an hour ride ahead of me, so click on my Spotify app and listened to my favorite playlist while I waited for the driver to show up.

Chapter 9

Mother's Day...

The airplane experienced a little turbulence a few miles outside city limits, and this minor disturbance awakened Jasmine from her sleep. She looked at her watch that read ten minutes past eleven as she yawned. She had a window seat on the right side of the plane, and the young woman to her left was hammering away on her laptop. There was a small baby crying due to the change in altitude, and Jasmine also felt her ears pop.

The pilot made the announcement that the plane was making its descent toward Midway Airport, and the seat belt light was turned on. The flight attendant instructed everyone to turn off their electronic devices as the plane drew near the airport. Jasmine looked to her left again and noticed a young man smiling at her. She smiled back at him for a brief moment and looked away.

The airplane landed about ten minutes later, and there was another ten-minute delay as passengers retrieved their luggage from the overhead cabin. She was one of the last passengers to exit the airplane because she was seated in the back. She finally stood up so that she could get her suitcase, and the young man who was smiling at her reached for it.

"Let me get that for you," the young man said.

"Thank you," Jasmine said.

They were the last two passengers to exit the plane, and they accompanied each other as they walked to baggage claim. Jasmine checked her cell phone to see if she had any calls or texts before placing it in her right back pocket. Nicole had sent her a text saying her plane had just landed. The young man observed the roundness and fullness of her backside as the phone barely fit inside her pocket. He also noticed her ultra-feminine gait, the bounciness of her long black hair, her smooth caramel complexion, and her captivating smile. Jasmine was what the brothers would call a dime-piece.

"I'm James, but my friends call me Jamie," he said.

"Nice to meet you, Jamie," she said. "My name is Jasmine."

"It's a pleasure to meet you, too, Jasmine. Can I take you out to lunch? My car is parked in the lot."

"No, thank you, Jamie. I'm meeting my sister here in a few minutes."

"Okay. Maybe some other time, then?"

Damn, he's so thirsty, she thought. She was used to men constantly hitting on her, and normally, she could always come up with an excuse to ward off a typical guy's advances. However, she wasn't prepared for Jamie's late-morning onslaught.

She then quickly looked him up and down. Nothing really stood out about him, but he was at least slightly taller than her, standing an inch or two above six feet. However, his fade needed a touch-up, and his Nikes were dingy looking. He was also very slim and had razor bumps on his face, and he was what a woman would consider average looking.

"Thanks, but no thanks, Jamie," she answered. "I just got out of a four-year relationship with my boyfriend, and I'm not ready to date anyone yet."

Breaking up with her boyfriend wasn't exactly a lie—they did end their relationship almost a year ago, but she had gone out on a few dates since then. Needless to say, she wasn't attracted to Jamie and was turned off by his over-eagerness.

"Oh, okay," he said, looking disappointed. "Well, you have a nice day."

"You, too, Jamie," she said as he walked on the other side of baggage claim.

That was close, she thought. She then glanced at Jamie on the other side of the baggage claim carousel, and he still had a disgusted look on his face and wouldn't look in her direction. She didn't take pleasure in rejecting guys who approached her on a consistent basis, and she felt bad about bruising Jamie's ego. However, in order for her to be able to function with any sense of normalcy, rejecting him was a necessary evil. She didn't rate him at the very bottom of the social ladder, but he was pretty close. He could've been a millionaire for all she knew, but she didn't choose a mate based solely on material things. In fact, she basically judged all men on three main traits, and none of them had anything to do with money.

The number one thing that a guy had to have was charisma—he had to have the confidence and intelligence to navigate his way around any situation, and most of all, he had to be able to protect her. Secondly, he had to be a God-fearing man—someone who wouldn't do anything immoral or unethical in the eyes of the Lord. And last but not least, the guy had to be attractive—he had to have the right height because she was five foot eleven, and he had to be cute and be in shape. Her list was, of course, longer than three requirements, but everything else was negotiable or even optional because she felt that a man with potential could acquire some the lesser traits that she desired in a man over a period of time. However, if a man didn't possess any one of these three main attributes, it was a deal-breaker for her.

She grabbed her phone out of her back pocket and sent Nicole a text telling her to meet up in baggage claim. Nicole's plane from Washington D.C. touchdown in Chicago a few minutes after Jasmine's plane from Los Angeles landed. Nicole arrived in baggage claim two minutes after Jasmine texted her.

"Hey, girl," Jasmine said, giving Nicole a firm hug. "I missed you so much."

"I missed you, too," Nicole said. "You still waiting on your bags, huh?"

"Yeah, they haven't started the carousel yet."

"Why is that guy over there mean-mugging you?"

"Girl, he was sweating me from the moment the plane landed. He asked me out and everything...hell, I thought he was about to propose to me. I tried to let him down easy though...I don't get off on hurting a guy's feelings."

"I hear you, but what are you supposed to do, Jaz? You can't date every single guy who asks you out. Believe me, I definitely know the feeling. The difference between me and you is that I stopped trying to spare these guys' feelings."

"That's cold, Nikki."

"It's the truth, Jaz."

"Did you send Mom a Mother's Day card?" Jasmine asked, changing the subject. "I hope she got mine...I mailed it on Wednesday."

"She probably got it, and yes, I sent her a card on Monday," Nicole answered. "We should take her out today."

"That's a great idea. We can to go to Dad's house after we take Mom out to dinner because Brock's already there."

"No, we'll go over there on Monday. We can stay with Mom tonight."

"I don't know about that, Nikki. I don't like her husband—he seems kind of creepy."

"I hear you on that. I get that same creepy vibe, too—like he's looking me up and down or something, but we can't leave Mom out in the cold on Mother's Day."

"Okay, but I'm only doing this for you."

"Thanks, Sis. I'm going to go get my suitcase."

"I'll be right here."

Nicole walked toward the baggage claim belt that had the flight information from Washington D.C. She was every bit as attractive as Jasmine, and they favored each other in looks greatly. They could literally pass for biological sisters because Brent married the same type of woman twice, as both wives had similar features and were very beautiful. The only slight differences between Jasmine and Nicole physically were their heights and complexions—Nicole was three inches shorter than Jasmine at five foot eight, but Nicole's legs were just as long as Jasmine's legs. Nicole was a shade lighter than Jasmine, and her best attribute was her captivating smile just like Jasmine's.

Nicole not only had the looks; she was also highly intelligent. She'd been a child prodigy who'd finished high school at fifteen years old and Georgetown undergrad at nineteen. She'd finished law school and was hired by the largest law firm in the Baltimore, Washington D.C., area by the age of twenty-one, and she'd made partner there at twenty-six. Even though she was close in age to her siblings, she was light-years ahead of them socially and in worldly experience.

Jasmine retrieved her luggage first and walked toward the baggage claim carousel where Nicole was standing. Nicole's luggage came out about ten minutes later, and they walked outside to the rideshare area. Jasmine requested an Uber on her app and began texting afterwards.

"What are you doing?" Nicole asked.

"I just sent Brock a text to meet us at Mom's house," Jasmine answered.

"Cool. Now we have to decide where we're going to eat."

"Yeah, we can wait until we all meet up at Mom's before we pick a place."

Their Uber arrived five minutes later, as there were dozens of passengers waiting in the rideshare area. Their mom lived in Homewood, a south suburb of Chicago.

"Hello, ladies," the driver said.

"Hi," Jasmine said, and Nicole didn't speak.

Nicole put her earphones on and shut her eyes. Jasmine began reading her novel, and the trip to Homewood was about a half-hour.

Chapter 10

"What do you got going on today?" I asked.

"Nothing," Malik answered. "What's up?"

"Do you wanna hang out with me and my sisters and take my stepmom out to lunch for Mother's Day?"

"Yeah, sure. What restaurant are we going to?"

"I don't know yet, but we're going to meet them at my stepmom's house in Homewood."

"Cool...I'm down for whatever."

"Damn, I want to go, too," Junior said. "I can't wait to get this damn monitor off my ankle."

"Don't worry. We all will have plenty of time to hang out with each other," I said.

"Yeah, I'll bring you something back from whatever restaurant we go to," Malik said.

"Thanks, I appreciate it," Junior said.

"I'll drive," I said, "and I'll meet you outside in a few minutes."

"Okay," Malik said.

Malik went outside, and I went upstairs to talk to my stepdad. His door was open, and he was studying the Bible.

"Hey, Dad, can I talk to you for a minute?" I asked.

"Sure, Brock," he answered. "What is it?"

I shut the door and answered, "I know who was responsible for what happened last week."

"Yeah? Who was it?"

"I ran into my ex-girlfriend Michelle last night at a club, and she told me that Will hangs out with the guys who robbed me and kidnapped you."

"And how does she know this? Can she prove it?"

"I'm pretty sure it was Will because Michelle said that her friend messes around with him on and off, and her friend also said that the two guys he hangs out with were from Compton."

"Wow, I need to call Stanton and give him this update. What are their names?"

"Michelle described them perfectly—she said Russell was the slim, dark-skinned one with the light brown eyes; and Terrence was the tall and muscular light-skinned one…"

"I'm going to call him right now."

My stepdad called Stanton, but his phone went to voice mail after five rings. He then left Stanton a message to call him.

"You don't seem all that surprised about Will," I said.

"I'm not," he said.

"You never liked him, huh?"

"Not really…I should've let him rot in jail back then. I was just waiting for you to see him for what he really is."

"BJ pretty much said the same thing."

He took a breath and said, "Stanton came by to see me last night, and I gave him their license plate number. He also filed a police report and said he'll try to keep the robbery and kidnapping out of the press."

"Keeping it out of the press is the least of my worries now that I know the truth," I said. "I just want to bring these guys down and deal with the fallout afterwards."

"If I know Stanton, he's probably running their plates now as we speak—he's very thorough and rarely takes any time off."

"You can also give him Will's cell number and have Stanton check the cell towers to see if he can track his phone. He can also check Will's phone records to see every call he made and received between the time you got kidnapped up until now."

"You sure know a lot about cell towers and cross-referencing calls, Brock."

"I used to sell drugs, remember? I had to at least try to stay one step ahead of the police even though I ultimately got caught."

"Right, I almost forgot about that. You've come a long way."

I texted Will's cell phone number, address and the address of his barbershop to him and said, "I just sent you all of Will's information—Malik and I are meeting Jaz and Nikki at Mom's house and taking her out to lunch."

"When did they get in town?"

"Their planes just landed about fifteen minutes ago."

"Okay, that's great. Give Gwendolyn my love."

"Sure thing. Can I borrow your car?"

"Yeah, go ahead."

"Thanks, Dad."

"No problem, Son, and I'll keep calling Stanton until I reach him."

"Let's keep this between us, okay? I don't want Nikki or Jaz to know about this, and I hope we can put them all behind bars before the end of this week."

"I have to disagree with you on this, Brock. Everybody is a target—you, me, Junior, and your sisters. Hell, I wouldn't be surprised if Malik was now on their radar."

"Okay, Dad, you know best. You've been my age, but I've never been yours."

"This is true. See you later, Son."

"Bye, Dad. Keep me posted."

"Okay, will do."

I went downstairs and said goodbye to Junior, and Malik was waiting for me outside standing next to my stepfather's car.

"You ready to go?" I asked.

"Yeah, let's do it," Malik answered.

"How was the party last night?" I asked as I pulled out the driveway.

"It was all right," Malik answered. "I stayed about an hour after you left."

"Yeah? How come you left so soon?"

"I wasn't feelin' it after a while. You got me thinking about all these women at the party chasing our fame and fortune."

"You had your light bulb moment, huh?"

"Yeah, you can say that. The girl who was giving me the most attention seemed to be only interested in trying to get in our circle. She wants to be an actress, so she started asking me if I knew certain people because she's looking for a break on the show *Empire*."

"So, she didn't really care about Malik, the person, right?"

"Exactly…and I told her that I couldn't help her because I didn't even live in Chicago or know anyone on the set of *Empire*."

"That's crazy…"

"Yeah, tell me about it. Sleeping with girls because of our celebrity is cool, but it gets old after a while. It would be nice if a woman wanted me for me."

"No doubt."

I took a breath and said, "I hope things work out with Naomi and me—we had a connection with each other before I made it to the NBA."

"I'm truly happy for you, and I hope things work out for you, too."

"Thanks, Malik. There's someone out there for you, but you have to be patient and stay faithful."

"Yeah, you may be on to something."

Malik paused and asked, "Your stepmom is your stepdad's first wife?"

"Yeah, she's Junior and Nikki's mom," I answered, "but she's also like a mom to me and Jaz. She was there for us when our mom died."

"So, she's still cool with your stepdad, huh?"

"Yeah, they're good friends—Dad was even at my stepmom's wedding a few years ago."

"Word? Your stepmom's married?"

"Yep, she's married to a car salesman who works at a Lexus dealership in Orland Park, and his name is Robert Reeves."

My stepmom had met Robert the same day Nicole and I had taken her to buy a new car. She hadn't wanted a new house, but she'd needed a new car. Nicole and I had split the cost and paid cash on her brand-new Lexus a couple of years ago. Needless to say, Robert had won her over with his charm, and they'd been inseparable ever since then.

"Nikki and Jaz don't care for him too much, though," I continued.

"Why not?"

"They view him as a slick car salesman who's not to be trusted."

"Do you trust him?"

"It's not important if I trust him or not because my stepmom does, and that's all that matters."

"That's real talk."

Malik rubbed his chin and asked, "Do Nikki and Jaz know about the robbery and abduction of your dad?"

"No, they don't," I answered. "And we're supposed to be having a surprise graduation party for Jaz on Friday."

"Oh, yeah? Do you think it's a good idea to still have the party on Friday?"

"I don't know, maybe not. I'm going to see if Nikki wants to push it back. If she doesn't, I'll have to come clean about our situation unless the cops arrest the guys involved."

"Yeah, it's probably best that we hold off for a while just in case they strike again."

"My mom can't stand our dad," Malik said, changing the subject after brief silence. "I remember her vividly, going back and forth to child support court for me and my brother and sister. He would quit a job and get another one in order to dodge the system, but they eventually caught up with him and forced him to pay."

"How do you feel about him?" I asked.

"I had resentment toward him, you know, but that was a long time ago. We since mended fences because I heard his side of the story."

"What legit reason did he have for avoiding to pay child support?"

"My mom wouldn't allow him to see us after they split, and after a period of time, he gave up. His logic was that he wasn't going to pay her and not be able to see us."

"And you're cool with that?"

"No, I'm not, but I chalked it up to both of them being very young and immature. I forgave him and my mom for their foolish choices."

"Yeah, I know all about forgiveness when it comes to my biological father. I was angry at him for years for his abusiveness toward me and my mom. The only thing that saved Jaz from the constant beatings was her age—she was only four years old when he got locked up."

"What did your dad do to get himself locked up?"

"He murdered this guy for cutting him off in traffic while he was on his way to work. Once my dad caught up to the guy at a stop light, he pulled out his gun and shot him in the head."

"Damn, talk about road rage…"

"I know, right? And it turned out that the guy he shot was somebody—the guy he killed was the son of a state senator."

"Really?"

"Yeah, it made the national news, and the only reason my father is still breathing is because Illinois doesn't have the death penalty. He ain't ever getting out of prison."

"Damn, that's messed up, Brock."

"I'm over it. Well—as over it as I can be."

"Have you seen him since then?"

"Yeah, I visited him for the first time after my second season in the NBA. Seeing him was all part of my maturation process—I was able to release my anger and forgive him for the abuse and abandonment."

"That's great, and your career took off after that."

"Yes, it did."

We were five minutes away from my stepmom's house, so I stopped at the Walgreens off of 183rd and Halsted to buy a Mother's Day card. The plan was to buy the card and get five hundred dollars out of the ATM.

"I'm gonna stop at this Walgreens to get my stepmom a card and some money," I said.

"Do your thing, man," Malik said. "I'll wait in the car."

Chapter 11

Naomi arrived at her mom's house in the Beverly area on the far south side of Chicago with a Mother's Day card and roses. Her older brother's car was already parked in front of their mom's house, so Naomi had to park farther down the block. *Damn, I hope he didn't bring his stuck-up wife with him*, she thought. She let herself in with her key moments later, and her brother Nicholas was sitting on the living room sofa watching television while their mom was in her room getting dressed.

"Hey, Nick, where's Mom?" Naomi asked.

"Hey, Nae, she's in her room getting dressed," Nicholas answered.

"Is she going somewhere?"

"Yeah, we were waiting on you so that we can all go out to eat."

"Where are we going?"

"Mom wants seafood, so she picked Red Lobster. We can go to the one in Orland Park."

"Okay, that's sounds great."

Naomi paused and asked, "Where's Candace?"

"She's taking her mother out to lunch for Mother's Day," Nicholas answered.

"Good."

"Don't be like that, Nae."

"Don't be like what? I just said that was good…"

"Whatever."

Nicholas had been an owner-operator truck driver for five years, making over two hundred grand a year. He was two years older than Naomi and had opted out of going to college once he'd graduated from high school. He also loved the open road and had been bitten by the bug the very first road trip the family had taken, to Wisconsin Dells. He'd gone to truck driving school shortly after graduation and been hired by a trucking company immediately after finishing the program. He'd then saved his money and boosted his credit score enough to buy his own rig in just two years, and the truck had paid for itself within the first year of being his own boss.

He met Candace last year and married her after dating only three months against the advice of his mother and Naomi because they were constantly at odds with each other—a match made in Hell, so to speak. Ultimately, getting married only made matters worse as they argued almost every other day. Nicholas was the quiet, nice guy type who would do just about anything to please the woman he loved. Candace, on the other hand, was the spoiled princess type who usually got her way and would nag and complain when she didn't. She was a succubus in the flesh—a hypergamous maneater whose greed and arrogance knew no bounds.

Candace viewed Nicholas as a simp, and she said 'I do' mainly because being married to him had its perks. He was on the road a great deal of the time which meant she had a lot of alone time to spend his money on clothes, pedicures, and fine dining, to name a few things. Naomi felt that she was using her brother and would dump him in a heartbeat if the right guy came into the picture.

Their mother's name was Natasha Hill. She was a beautiful, fifty-year-old ex-personal banker who'd lost her job after the stock market crash during Obama's first presidential term. She'd nearly lost everything after that—their house, her car, and her marriage—Naomi and Nicholas's father had left, as the struggle to maintain the house with his salary alone was too much to bear. However, their mom had been able to bounce back a few years later by totally reinventing herself and doing what she was meant to do as a chef for an upscale restaurant downtown, and their father had remarried and was still an important part of his children's lives.

"Hi, baby," Natasha said to Naomi as she came out her room.

"Happy Mother's Day, Mom," Naomi said as she greeted her mother with a hug and a kiss.

"Thank you, sweetheart," Natasha said. "I'll put these roses in some water."

"Are you ready to go, Mom?" Nicholas asked.

"Yes, I am," Natasha answered. "I hope Lobsterfest is still going on, because I want to order the steak and lobster combo."

"I think what you want is the Admiral Feast, and they serve it all year 'round," Naomi said. "I'm going to get the all-you-can-eat shrimp if they have it."

"Let's get going because I'm starving," Natasha said.

They all left the house shortly afterwards, and Nicholas volunteered to drive to the restaurant. Everyone in the city of Chicago seemed to be out that afternoon, and there was road construction eastbound on 111th Street.

"Did you make a reservation, Nick?" Naomi asked.

"No, I didn't," Nicholas answered. "We couldn't decide on where we wanted to go right away."

"The restaurant is probably going to be packed," Naomi said.

"No worries," Natasha said. "If we can't get in, we can try Dustie's in Matteson. Soul food is my second choice."

"You can have whatever you like, Mom," Nicholas said.

They arrived at Red Lobster about thirty minutes later, and the parking lot was almost filled to capacity. Nicholas pulled up in front of the entrance, and Naomi said, "I'll go inside and try to reserve us a table or booth."

Naomi hopped out the car and went inside. There were several people standing, and all of the seats were taken. She asked the hostess the wait time for being seated somewhere. The young lady told her that it could be anywhere from a twenty to forty-five-minute wait, so she told the hostess to put her name on the list. It was then that she noticed Candace and another man, sitting at a booth, eating and conversing. She stepped a little closer to the dining area to make sure that it was indeed Candace and her beau indulging in forbidden fruit.

She pulled out her phone from her back pocket and snapped a couple of photos of them and said to the hostess, "Never mind. You can take my name off the list."

"Okay, have a nice day," the hostess said politely.

"Thank you," Naomi said as she quickly exited the restaurant.

She spotted Nicholas and their mom walking toward the front entrance of the restaurant from the north end of the parking lot and gestured to them to hold up.

"What's wrong?" Nicholas asked.

"It's too crowded," Naomi answered. "There's an hour wait, so let's go to Dustie's."

"Fine by me," Natasha said.

"Okay, let's do it," Nicholas said.

Chapter 12

Will grabbed three beers out the fridge and came back to the living room area and handed Russell and Terrence one each. He then turned the television onto an NBA playoff game. Russell lit a cigarette and took a puff before blowing some smoke out of his nostrils.

"What's the plan, fam?" Will asked.

"Our prime targets are Malik and Brock's sister Nikki," Terrence answered. "We know that Malik banks with Chase, right?"

"Right," Will answered.

"And Chase will allow you to transfer up to 250 grand per day through online banking," Terrence stated. "We'll make Malik wire the money into my offshore account, and once the money clears, it can sit there until we get settled in Windsor."

"So, we gonna settle down in Canada?" Will asked.

"Yep, that's the plan," Russell answered. "Is your passport current?"

"Yeah, it's current," Will affirmed.

"Let's assume that Nikki's bank has the same policy," Terrence continued, "and we'll hit her up the exact same way. I'll use my phone to do the wire transfer."

"What if they don't do online banking?" Will asked. "I know that I don't do anything online."

"It will take all of five minutes to open up an online profile," Terrence answered. "It's 2018, fam…you really need to get with the times."

"I'm good, bro," Will said.

"Welcome to the Dark Ages," Russell added.

"How are we gonna take the money across the border?" Will asked.

"We will each launder our cut of the money at one of the casinos in northwest Indiana, and they will write us each a cashier's check when we cash out," Terrence answered. "We might have to blow five or ten grand each in order to make everything look legit."

"We should split up and go to different casinos," Russell stated.

"You're right," Terrence said. "I'll go the Blue Chip Casino in Michigan City…"

"And I'll go to the Majestic Star Casino in Gary," Russell said.

"I guess it'll be the Horseshoe Casino for me," Will said.

"And we'll back each other up at each casino just in case some crew tries to rob us," Terrence said.

Russell paused and then said, "So, five hundred grand split three ways, plus the one million we got courtesy of Brock and Malik, puts us at five hundred grand apiece."

"Yeah, we'll be comfortable," Terrence said, "but I'm gonna open up my own business."

"And what business is that?" Will asked.

"I'm gonna start a lawn care service," Terrence answered. "I'm second to none when it comes to landscaping."

"That's what's up, Terry," Will said. "As y'all probably already know, I'm gonna open up another barbershop…haircuts are what I do best."

"What about you, Russ?" Terrence asked.

"I don't know," Russell answered. "What I do know is that y'all could've done what y'all planning on doing right here in the US without robbing Brock and Malik. I want to do something different."

"And what's that?" Will asked.

"Maybe I'll go back to school," Russell answered. "I'll do what I should've done in the first place instead of choosing the military."

"What will you major in?" Terrence asked.

"Computer science, you know, something tech-related," Russell answered.

"Sounds like a great plan, man," Terrence said.

Russell took a swig of his beer and put out his cigarette in the ashtray on the living room table and said, "What about your girl, Sherita? Are you gonna take her with you?"

"Hell, no," Terrence answered. "Our relationship has run its course, and I'm done with her. All she does is argue and nag me every chance she gets."

"Yeah, there's nobody keeping me here either," Russell said.

"Does Sherita know your plans?" Will asked. "She can throw a monkey wrench in our program."

"Don't worry, Will. She doesn't know a damn thing," Terrence answered. "What about you? Do you have anybody close to you?"

"Nah, all I do is stick and move, man," Will answered. "Both of my parents are dead, and there's nobody special keeping me here. I'm gonna leave my house to my little sister because she's got three kids."

"What about your barbershop?" Terrence asked.

"I'm gonna let Calvin run it from now on," Will answered.

"It sounds like all of us are starting with a clean slate," Terrence said as he raised his beer bottle and Russell and Will followed suit. "Here's to new beginnings."

"To new beginnings," Russell added.

"I'll drink to that," Will said.

Chapter 13

Malik and I arrived at my stepmom's house shortly after I bought her Mother's Day card from Walgreens. I proceeded to park in her driveway and rang the doorbell once we step foot on the porch. Jasmine opened the door, and I greeted her with a big hug.

"I've missed you, little sis," I said after I kissed her on the cheek.

"I've missed you, too, Brock," Jasmine said.

"You remember Malik, don't you?" I asked.

"Of course I do," Jasmine answered as she gave Malik a warm embrace. "Nice to see you again."

"Likewise," Malik said.

"Hey, Nikki," I said as I gave her a hug and kiss on the cheek also.

"Hey, Brock," Nicole said. "What's Dad up to?"

"You know, studying the Bible," I answered.

"Yeah, it is Sunday," Nicole said.

"Sorry about you guys' loss in the playoffs," Nicole said as she greeted Malik with a hug.

"Thanks, we'll get them next year," Malik said.

"Where's Mom?" I asked.

"She's still getting dressed," Jasmine said.

"Where does Mom want to eat?" I asked.

"Nowhere in particular," Nicole answered, "but she wants the fine dining experience like we just had when you were in D.C. a month ago."

"You two went out to dinner and didn't tell me about it?" Jasmine asked.

"It was spur of the moment," I answered. "We were in town to play the Wizards, and Nikki and I hooked up afterwards. Besides, I treated you to dinner both times when we were in L.A. for the Lakers and the Clippers games."

"Yeah, Jaz, you don't hear me whining about you all going out twice," Nicole said.

"I'm just sayin', it would've been nice if all three of us hung out, that's all," Jasmine said.

"It sounds like you all had a great time on each occasion," Malik chimed in. "Thanks for inviting me today, Brock."

"No problem, bro," I said.

"We're gonna take good care of you, Malik," Jasmine added as she smiled and winked at him.

"Thank you, Jasmine," Malik said.

"You're very welcome," Jasmine said.

"Where's Robert?" I asked.

"Thankfully, out with his mother," Jasmine answered.

"Still not a fan of his, huh?" I asked.

"You can say that," Jasmine answered.

"What about you, Nikki?" I asked.

"No comment," she answered.

My stepmom came downstairs a few minutes later and greeted everyone. I handled her the Mother's Day card with five crisp one-hundred-dollar bills inside and gave her a hug and kiss on the cheek. I then said, "Dad sends his love."

"Thank you for the card, baby," Gwendolyn said. "How's Brent doing?"

"He's good," I answered.

"And you must be Malik," Gwendolyn said. "I've heard so much about you."

Malik gave her a hug and said, "Nice to meet you, Missus…"

"You can call me Gwen," Gwendolyn said.

"Nice to meet you, Gwen," Malik said.

"Nice to meet you as well," Gwendolyn said.

Gwendolyn Reeves was a beautiful, forty-eight-year-old high school English teacher who didn't look a day over thirty. In fact, Gwendolyn, Nicole, and Jasmine could all pass for sisters.

"Where do you want to eat, Mom?" Nicole asked.

"I know it's probably too late to make a reservation, but I'd like to go to 94 West."

"I'm sure that Malik or I can get us in without a reservation," I said.

"Definitely me," Malik said. "Brock has no game."

"Whatever, man," I said.

"We're gonna see what you're made of," Nicole said. "Twenty bucks says you can't get us a reservation."

"I'm with Nikki," I said. "Twenty says they turn us back around. Mom, what do you think?"

"That's between you guys," Gwendolyn said. "All that I want to do is eat, and any place will do at this point."

"I've got twenty on Malik getting us in," Jasmine said. "You'll definitely win them over with that smile of yours."

"See there, somebody has confidence in me," Malik said.

We all barely fit inside of my stepdad's car and headed to 94 West in Orland Park. I picked up on the vibe that Jasmine had a crush on Malik, and my initial reservations about him had disappeared because of the fact he'd put his life on the line for me and my stepdad. I had considered him family from that point on and would give them my blessing if they chose to be in a committed relationship with each other.

I found a parking space in the farthest spot from the front entrance of the restaurant, and it was time for Malik to work his magic. The hostess greeted us, and there was a lively crowd inside.

"We don't have a reservation, but I was hoping that you still would be able to accommodate us," Malik said.

"You can speak with my manager, but I can't promise anything," the hostess said. "We're booked until closing."

"Okay, that's fair," Malik said.

The hostess dialed her manager's extension and told him the situation. She hung up the phone and said, "He'll be out shortly."

"Okay, thanks," I said. "It's not looking good."

"Let's just see what the manger says," Malik said.

"It's last-minute," Nicole said, "and I should've reserved something earlier last week."

"We're sorry, Mom," Jasmine added. "All of us should be ashamed of ourselves."

"If we can't get a table here, it's okay," Gwendolyn said.

"Don't worry, Mom, if we can't reserve something, we'll get a reservation somewhere else," I said.

The manager walked up to us and asked, "What can I do for you guys?"

"I was hoping we'd get lucky," Malik answered. "Do you have any cancellations or latecomers?"

"Let me check the guest list," the manager answered.

The manager scanned the guest list for several seconds, and after careful review, he said, "I'm sorry, folks. I have no cancellations, and I only have one customer who called ahead and is running fifteen minutes late."

"Okay, thank you for checking," Malik said.

The manager subsequently examined Malik carefully, and then he looked at me before asking, "Hey, don't you guys play for the St. Louis Wolves?"

"Yes, we do," Malik said, his grin widening. "I'm Malik Thomas."

"I know," the manager said. "My name is Grayson, and I'm a huge fan."

"Nice to meet you," Malik said as he shook Grayson's hand.

He extended his hand to me, and I said, "I'm Brock...nice to meet you."

"Can I have both your autographs?" Grayson asked.

"Sure," I said.

"And I'm Nicole Jones," Nicole said jokingly.

"Girl, you're crazy," Jasmine said.

"Why didn't you all say something?" Grayson asked.

"We didn't want to use our celebrity in order to bump someone off the list," Malik answered.

"Luckily, I have the banquet room available for you," Grayson said. "We just finished cleaning up after the family who reserved it earlier this afternoon left, and it's yours if you want it."

"Yes, we will take it," I said. "Thank you."

"No problem," Grayson said. "Come this way."

We followed Grayson to the banquet room, and he led us to the long table in the front of the room next to the podium. A reservation for the banquet room normally had a twenty-five person minimum, but Grayson accommodated us anyway.

"I want my twenty bucks from the both of you," Malik said.

"Technically, you dropped the ball," I said. "If it wasn't for the fact that Grayson recognized us, we'd be searching for somewhere else to eat."

"Brock has a point," Nicole said.

"No, a bet is a bet," Jasmine interjected. "It doesn't matter how Malik did it—the point is that he reserved our table."

"Thank you, Jasmine," Malik said. "I'm glad someone appreciates my efforts."

"I got your back," Jasmine said.

"I definitely appreciate you, Malik," Gwendolyn said. "Let's just order because I'm starving."

Chapter 14

Detective Stanton was on his way to the address that the license plate was registered—a three-flat apartment building in the Auburn Gresham neighborhood on the southwest side of Chicago. The car was registered in Sherita Miller's name—Terrence's ex-girlfriend. They'd broken up after a heated argument that took place the morning after Terrence had failed to come home or call. Sherita had called the police once their verbal exchange escalated to becoming physical, and Terrence hadn't been back to her apartment since then. In fact, Terrence and Sherita's relationship had been volatile since its inception over three years ago, and Terrence had spent several nights in the bullpen due to domestic violence toward her.

Stanton rang Sherita's bell on her mailbox and got no response at first. He rang the doorbell again thirty seconds later, and she buzzed him in. Her apartment was on the top floor, and she was waiting for him when he came upstairs to the third floor.

"Who are you?" she asked.

"I'm Detective Stanton, ma'am," he answered after he flashed his badge, "and are you Sherita Miller, correct?"

"Yeah…what do you want?"

"I need you to answer some questions."

Sherita was the epitome of a butterface—a young woman who led a fast life, and every mistake that she made in life manifested in her appearance. She was brash and sassy, and her contentious disposition made a lasting impression on Stanton.

"What the hell is this about?" she asked sarcastically.

"I need to know who owns the vehicle with the license plates 'MR GRIM'?" he answered.

"That would be my trifling ex-boyfriend."

"Does he have a name?"

"Yeah, his name is Terrence Chandler."

"Do you know where I can find him?"

"No, I don't. We broke up about three months ago, and I haven't seen or heard from him since then."

"Why did you all break up?"

"He beat the hell outta me, and I called the cops on him."

"So, he has a warrant out on him, huh?"

"Yes."

"Does he have a crew?"

"Yes, he runs with guys named Russell Martin and Will Johnson."

"Do you know where they live?"

"Not exactly…I've been to Will's house once. He stays on 88th and Luella, but I don't know the exact address."

Stanton paused for a moment and said, "Here's my card. Call me if you can think of anything else that might help me find him."

"What did he do this time if you don't mind me asking?" she asked.

"Terrence is a suspect in a robbery and kidnapping," he answered.

"It figures. He's always into something."

"And what is that?"

"He runs drugs out of his friend Will's barbershop on 79th and Constance."

"I see. Thank you for your help, Sherita."

"You're welcome. Terrence is an animal and needs to be off the streets before he hurts somebody else."

"Indeed he does. I'll be in touch."

Stanton left Sherita's apartment and decided to go back to the station to wrap up things for the day. He just uncovered a new lead in the case, and Will was his ace in the hole that was going to lead him to the other two members of the crew.

He checked his phone before he drove off and saw that Brent called and left a message. He then listened to his voice mail, and he called Brent afterwards.

"Hey, Brent," Stanton said. "What you got?"

"Brock found out through a friend that his friend Will was directly responsible for robbery and kidnapping," Brent answered.

"I found out the same thing," Stanton said. "The ex-girlfriend of one of the kidnappers told me that they run drugs out of Will's barbershop on 79th and Constance."

"Brock wanted me to give you Will's cell phone...he figured you could find the other two guys numbers on his call log."

"That's a good idea. Now I have enough to arrest each one of them and bring them in for questioning, and I can get a warrant to search Will's house and barbershop after I check his phone records."

"How soon will you be able to arrest them?"

"I won't be able to start doing anything until sometime tomorrow. I'll have the phone company fax me Will's records first thing in the morning."

"Good. Keep me posted."

"You bet. Talk to you later, Brent."

"Later, Blaine."

Chapter 15

June and Cecilia lay blissfully in each other's arms on the living room sofa watching television and hadn't left June's apartment since Saturday evening after they hashed things out at Ronnie's Steakhouse downtown. They'd been able to clear up any misunderstandings between them, and they had been making love ever since then. The only time they came up for air was to use the bathroom and shower.

June lived in Calumet City in south suburban Chicago, and he had been with the CTA since dropping out of college after his third year, as he only had enough credits to be classified as a sophomore. He'd realized then that he wasn't built for college and opted to stay on as a bus driver full-time, after being in their summer program for students.

"I've missed you so much, Cecilia," he said, kissing her on the forehead. "A day doesn't go by without me thinking about you."

"I was so angry at you for a long time," she said, "but I realize now that I was angry for no reason other than fate dealing us a bad hand. I've missed you, too, and I thought I'd never see you again."

"I love you, and I always have since I met you."

"I love you, too, June, and I'm never going to let you go."

"Thank God I found you."

"So, you think my girl Naomi is pretty, huh?" she asked jokingly, changing the subject.

"She's all right, but she ain't got nothing on you, baby," he answered.

"Yeah, right," she said, tapping him lightly on his leg. "I bet you'd all over her if I wasn't in the picture."

"I'm not gonna lie," he said. "I was feelin' her for a while, but I realized that I wasn't her type after she kept blowing me off."

"How do you feel about her now? Naomi is beautiful, and she's a great catch."

"I'm over it, sweetheart. I only have eyes for you, so you have nothing to worry about."

"That's good to know, June."

There was brief silence before he asked, "Where do we go from here?"

"What do you mean?"

"What does the future hold for us? I mean, you're in Michigan, and I'm here in Chicago. I want us to be together every day, but that's not going to be possible."

"We'll figure it out, baby. I don't know where I'll end up now that I'm done with my residency, and besides, Illinois has many opportunities for doctors to serve in distressed areas of the state."

"Well, I'll do the long-distance thing if I have to, because I don't want to lose you again."

"You're not going to lose me, June—not on your life."

"You're not gonna hang out with your mother today?" he asked, changing the subject again.

"My sister texted me and said the entire family went out for bunch earlier," she answered. "I'll just have to make it up to her somehow."

"When do you have to be back in Michigan?"

"I don't leave until Wednesday, and I still haven't spent any time with my girl."

"I sorry—I didn't mean to alter your plans..."

"It's not your fault. We had no idea that we'd run into each other."

"I'll tell you what. I can take you home so that you can spend some time with your mom and Naomi, and I'll make sure I see you before you leave."

"What if I don't want to leave?"

"I would love nothing more than to keep you here with me until your flight leaves, but I'd feel guilty about monopolizing your time."

"Well, okay, since you put it that way. If I send you a plane ticket to Grand Rapids, will you come?"

"Of course I will, baby, but I can buy my own plane ticket. All I needed was an invitation."

"Okay, Mister Wonderful, you just got one."

Chapter 16

Dinner with my sisters and stepmom was great. The food was good, the conversation amongst all of us was pleasant and interesting, and Jasmine made it obvious that she had feelings for Malik. Her overt affection toward him made him slightly uneasy as he tried his very best to be respectful to the family by not openly acknowledging her advances. He, in fact, probably felt that Jasmine was a little too young and inexperienced for him, or maybe he felt the same way she felt but was too embarrassed to admit it.

Malik and I arrived back at the house, and Nicole and Jasmine opted to stay at my stepmom's house for the night. I put the car in park but left the engine running.

"My sister has a huge crush on you, Malik," I said.

"Yeah, it seems that way," Malik said reluctantly. "I didn't quite know how to react to that."

"I know—I could tell the whole situation made you feel a little uncomfortable."

"It's cool, though. I didn't want to be disrespectfully or anything—Jaz is a beautiful girl, and any man would be lucky to have her."

"Yes, she is. Jaz is a virgin, you know, and that's the main reason why her college sweetheart broke up with her."

"No, I didn't know that."

"Jaz is of the ninety-ninth percentile—she's one of the very few virtuous women left who's saving herself for marriage."

"Well, that's great. You don't have to worry about me trying to deflower your sister—I took what you said to heart on the plane ride here. I would never hurt Jaz."

"Don't even sweat that, Malik. I know you wouldn't do anything to hurt Jaz. Come on, let's go inside."

I turned the engine off, and we went inside the house. Malik brought Junior some food home as promised—a ribeye steak with a salad and baked potato. Junior was in his usual spot on the living room sofa watching television when we got back. I quickly checked my phone and saw that Naomi texted me:

I was just thinking about you. Can't wait to see you tomorrow.

"What's up, fellas?" Junior asked.

"I'm stuffed like a Thanksgiving turkey," I answered.

"I brought you some food, bro," Malik answered. "I hope you like rib-eye steak, and I got you a salad and a baked potato."

"Good looking out, fam," Junior said. "I'm starving."

"No problem," Malik said.

I texted Naomi backed and said:

Just got back from dinner with my sisters and stepmom and Malik. I can't wait to see u 2.

"Who are you texting?" Junior asked while warming up his food in the microwave.

"Damn, man, all in my business," I answered. "I was texting Naomi, if you must know."

"Brock's in love," Junior said jokingly.

"That may be, but when are we going to meet this Melissa?" I asked.

"You have a girlfriend?" Malik asked.

"Yes, I have a girlfriend," Junior answered, "and you will meet her at Jaz's surprise graduation party, Brock."

I shook my head and said, "I don't about that, BJ."

"You don't know about what?" Junior asked. "The party is still on, isn't it?"

"We might have to hold off on the party because of the current situation," I answered, "but I haven't talked to Nikki yet. As far as I know, she still plans to surprise Jaz on Friday."

"Oh, okay," Junior said. "Did you tell Nikki and Jaz about what happened?"

"Not yet," I answered. "I didn't want to say anything at dinner today."

"Nikki's gonna go off if she doesn't hear it from you first," Junior said.

"I know," I said.

"How long are you gonna be in town?" Junior asked Malik.

"I'll be here until Saturday," Malik answered. "My flight leaves for New York at five in the evening."

"Going home to see the family, huh?" I asked.

"Yep, I'm gonna hang out with my mom and brother for a few days before I return to St. Louis," Malik answered.

"Jaz's gonna hate to see you go," I said.

"I'm sure I'll be back to see all of you before the season starts," Malik said.

"What's up with you and Jaz?" Junior asked Malik.

"Nothing much," Malik answered. "We're just getting to know each other."

"Jaz has a crush on our boy," I said.

"Word?" Junior asked. "That's great, man. She needs to be with somebody cool like you, fam. I didn't care for her last boyfriend."

"Yeah, Rick was a character," I added. "It was good that they broke up when they did. I was getting tired of him pressuring Jaz to have sex with him before she was ready."

"He's lucky I was locked up because I would've paid him a visit," Junior said.

"He sounds like a real jerk," Malik said.

"Let's just say that nobody was happy to see him at any of the family functions," I said.

Rick May was Jasmine's boyfriend in high school and college. They'd gone to separate schools—he'd attended the University of Illinois while Jasmine had been on the west coast at USC— but they'd maintained a long-distance relationship up to the end of their junior year. Jasmine had hoped he'd propose by then, but she'd found out that Rick had been seeing other women behind her back. Needless to say, her trust had been broken, and they'd decided it would be in their best interests to end the relationship before the start of their senior year.

"He broke her heart, huh?" Malik asked.

"Yeah, and she didn't take it too well," I answered. "I made sure I talked to her at least twice a week to lift her spirits and keep her mind on her studies."

"Jaz is lucky to have you," Malik said. "Anything you need for Jaz's party to run smoothly, just let me know."

"Thanks, bro, I appreciate that," I said.

Junior stood up from the kitchen table once he finished eating his food, and he threw his waste in the garbage before walking back to the living room area. It was then that Malik noticed how tall Junior was, as he was only about an inch or two shorter than I was because I had just gotten off the couch to go the kitchen.

"Did you play ball in high school?" Malik asked Junior.

"Yes, as a matter of fact, I did," Junior answered. "Why?"

"I just noticed how tall you are for the first time," Malik answered.

"I'm six foot three," Junior said, "but I wasn't all that quick and couldn't jump very high like Brock. I could light it up from the outside, though."

"Junior was a great baseball player, Malik," I added. "He had pro scouts coming to his games in high school."

"So, what happened, BJ?" Malik asked. "How come you're not playing in the majors?"

"I was stupid, bro," Junior answered. "I started running the streets and lost focus before I eventually dropped out of school."

"Don't even sweat that, bro," Malik said. "You'll figure it out."

"I hope so," Junior said.

Chapter 17

"Why were you sweatin' Malik so hard?" Nicole asked.

"Because he's everything I want in a man, Nikki," Jasmine answered. "The problem is that I don't think he's feelin' me like that."

"Girl, please...he isn't going anywhere. I can tell he's really into you by the way he looks at you, but let the man breathe."

"But what if he never asks me out?"

"Jaz, you're the prize. He'd be stupid not to ask you out."

"I'm just saying...he's so fine and tall. I'd melt if he wrapped his long arms and broad shoulders around me, and that smile of his..."

"It's sounds like you're just caught up in the way he looks. You don't know anything about him other than the fact that he plays in the NBA, and you don't even know if he has someone special back in St. Louis."

"I know, but I can't help the way I feel."

"Just let him come to you. Stop putting yourself out there like that."

"Okay, Nikki, you're right."

A few seconds later, Robert walked through the door, and their whole mood changed. He sensed the tension right away, but he didn't let it ruin his mood.

"Hello, ladies," Robert greeted them.

"Hi, Robert," Jasmine answered, but Nicole didn't say a word.

"How you doing, Nicole?" Robert asked, not letting her off the hook without speaking.

"Hello, Robert," Nicole in her formal, lawyer-like tone. "I'm going to crash, Jaz. I'll see you in the morning."

Nicole abruptly went into the guest room without looking back or uttering a single word. Jasmine proceeded to follow suit before Robert stopped her.

"Wait, Jasmine," he said.

"What is it, Robert?"

"I just wanted to tell you congratulations on graduating with honors."

"Thank you very much."

"And I got you a gift. Wait here, I'll be right back."

Jasmine sat back down on the love seat in the living room and waited patiently. Robert returned to the living room area moments later with a brown Michael Kors purse, and Jasmine's whole facial expression changed.

"I hear that young women are into Michael Kors bags, so I took the liberty of buying you one," he said.

"Wow!" she exclaimed, giving him a tight embrace, and he placed his right hand lightly on her upper back. "This was the exact purse I had my eye on last week. Thank you so much, Robert."

"You're very welcome, Jasmine."

He sighed and said, "I'm going to wind down with your stepmom in the bedroom. Goodnight."

"Goodnight, Robert, and thanks again."

He nodded, and she plopped back down in the love seat, completely flabbergasted. Maybe he's not so bad after all, she thought. She sat for a moment to gather her thoughts and take in what just happened, and then she went to the guest room to show off her new purse to Nicole.

"Check out what Robert just gave me for a graduation present," Jasmine said.

"Is that what you were screaming about?" Nicole asked.

"Yes, isn't it sharp? I've got so many outfits to match this purse with."

"Traitor…"

"Excuse me?"

"You heard what I said. All it takes is for some man to buy you something, and you get all giddy and brand-new on me."

"Whatever, Nikki…stop hatin'."

"I'm not hating on you, Jaz. You couldn't stand the man five minutes ago, now you're his biggest fan because he bought you a damn purse."

"Maybe we were wrong about him…"

"I'm so disappointed in you…I thought I schooled you better than that."

"Whatever…I'm going to watch television in the family room. Goodnight."

"Goodnight, traitor."

Chapter 18

Naomi was sitting at her desk in the corner of the living room trying to focus on studying for one of her final exams on Tuesday. However, what happened between Cecilia and June weighed heavily on her mind as well as the dilemma with her brother and his wife. She finally decided to close her book and lie down on the living room sofa instead. She waited for Cecilia to call her, because she didn't want to bother her while she tried to sort things out with June and decided it was best to just let the whole situation play out.

She shut her eyes as darkness began to set in on a cool Sunday night. The central air unit's heat in her apartment came on, and she dozed off before her phone rang.

"Hey, CeCe," Naomi said.

"Can you let me in?" Cecilia asked.

"Sure, hold on."

Naomi buzzed Cecilia in and left her door unlock for her. Cecilia came inside a minute later and said, "Hey, girl. I'm sorry we haven't had a chance to really hang out yet."

"Is everything okay?" Naomi asked.

"Yes, everything's great."

"You worked things out with June?"

"Yes, we're together now."

"That's wonderful, CeCe. I'm so happy for you guys."

"He took me back to his place, and we made love all night and most of the morning."

"Damn, girl…you're still able to walk?"

"Barely…we wore each other out."

"I just love a happy ending, and nobody deserves one more than you."

"He still loves me after all this time, and he wants to marry me."

"Marry you? But what do you want?"

"I don't know…I just finished medical school, and marriage was the furthest thing from my mind…"

"Do you love him?"

"Yes, Nae, I'm very much in love with him."

"Then you'll figure it out."

"But we're in two different cities right now, and I don't know where I'll end up next. I don't want him to quit his job for me."

"What's more important, being with June or a job?"

Cecilia didn't answer her, and Naomi said, "You already know the answer to that."

"One minute, I had my life planned out for the next five years, and now it's upside down," Cecilia said.

"You're worrying about nothing," Naomi said. "June came back in your life for a reason...so what if it wasn't in your plans?"

"Enough about me, Nae. What about you and Brock?"

"We're still on for tomorrow. Don't try to deflect the focus off you."

"But have you spoken to him today?"

"No, but we texted each other."

"A text?"

"We would've gone out today if hadn't made plans with a certain doctor fresh out of med school."

"Touché."

"You want to get some ice cream?" Naomi said cheerfully.

"Girl, no," Cecilia answered. "You know that I'm lactose-intolerant."

"Well, then, do you want to go to Dairy Queen with me so that *I* can get some ice cream?"

"Come on. Let's go before they close."

"You drove?"

"Yeah, I have June's car. Where's a Dairy Queen around here?"

"There's one on Torrence Avenue in Lansing. It's not that far."

"Do they sell hot dogs?"

"No, but they have burgers or chicken strips."

"Damn, I had a taste for a hot dog."

"Sonic sells hot dogs."

"No, thanks. I don't like Sonic."

They left Naomi's apartment complex and headed east on 159th Street to Torrence Avenue. Cecilia then made a right on Torrence onto Lansing.

"I need to tell you something," Naomi said before she sighed.

"This isn't about June, is it?"

"What? Hell no, CeCe."

"Then what is it?"

"Nicholas' wife Candace is cheating on him."

"What? How do you know this?"

"I saw her with her side-piece at Red Lobster today when I was with Nicholas and my mom."

"Wait, did Nicholas catch her in the act?"

"No, I was the only one who saw her. I went inside to make us a reservation while they parked the car, and that's when I saw Candace feeding her boo-thing a shrimp. Needless to say, I told my mom and Nicholas that the waiting time was too long and got the hell outta there."

"Wow, that's terrible."

"I don't know what to do."

"That's your brother, Nae. You have to tell him the truth."

"But how? He's going to hate me…"

"He'll hate you more if you don't tell him. Sure, he'll be mad at you for a while, but he'll appreciate that you told him the truth in the long run."

"What would I say to him?"

"Just tell him exactly what you saw. Don't let that skank off the hook."

"You're right. I'll tell sometime this week."

"Do you want me to come with you?"

"No, I should be okay."

They pulled up in front of Dairy Queen and parked in the lot.

"You sure you don't want anything?" Naomi asked.

Cecilia handed Naomi a twenty-dollar bill and said, "You can get me some chicken strips and get whatever you want."

"Okay, thanks. I'll be right back."

Chapter 19

Can two walk together, except they be agreed? Amos 3:3

I sat in front of Will's barbershop for what seemed like an eternity. I had thoughts of killing him amongst a dozen or so witnesses, but I was way too controlled to give into my primal thoughts. Besides, I had no concrete proof that he was directly involved in the kidnapping and robbery other than his association with Terrence and Russell. Our lives had taken completely different paths once we were released from Cook County jail some seven years ago, and it was like I had been holding on to a friendship that was long gone or never there in the first place.

The rental car that I chose smelled like stale cigarette smoke, and the sound system inside this mid-grade Chevy Malibu was of minimum standard quality. The first thing I was going to do after getting a touch-up was to go to a real car wash to get rid of the odor inside the rental. My stepdad had errands to run all morning, so I didn't want to impose on him by borrowing his car.

I took a sip of my coffee and continued to sit in front of Will's shop. What was I going to say to him, and how was I going to keep my cool? Two more patrons walked in, and the crowd was starting to pick up. It was decision time, so I didn't have the luxury of procrastinating any longer. Will was cutting someone's hair when I finally decided to enter the shop, and he smiled and gave me a pound when he saw me.

"Can you fit me in?" I asked.

"Yeah, bro, I can touch your fade up when I finish with the homie," he answered.

"Cool."

I sat down and listened to the barbershop banter while skimming through an ESPN magazine. One conversation going on was about the police brutality against Black men happening throughout the country, and two other guys were talking about the NBA playoffs while looking in my direction.

"Say, dude, aren't you Brock Lane?" one of the guys asked me.

"Yes, I am," I answered.

"Yeah, that's my boy," Will chimed in.

Oh, now I'm your boy, I thought to myself. I wasn't your boy when you were planning your damn heist. It was a struggle to keep my temper in check from that point on.

"I thought that was you," the guy said as he walked toward me to shake my hand. "I'm Nelson…can you sign my jersey?"

"Sure, no problem," I said. "Do you have a Sharpie?"

"Yes, I do," he said.

I signed his jersey and gave a few other patrons an autograph before sitting back down.

"Did you heard the rumors about Flash Tucker signing with the Wolves as an unrestricted free agent?" Nelson asked.

"No, I'm afraid I didn't hear about that," I answered. "I haven't watched any sports since losing to Houston in game seven."

"Yeah, it's been the topic of conversation all morning long on ESPN," he said. "He wants a max deal, but the Rockets don't want to pay him because he turns thirty in September."

"Well, we'll see what happens," I said.

I entertained that conversation longer than I wanted, but I had to keep up appearances for the sake of getting inside of Will's head before leaving his shop. I needed to know his motivation for betraying me without him getting wind of the fact that I was on to him.

Will was finally ready to cut my hair after a ten-minute wait, and the previous customer tipped him before I sat down in his chair. He then promptly placed a fresh towel around my neck and began cutting my hair.

"What's been up, Brock?" he asked.

"Nothing much," I said. "I'm still trying to wrap my mind around what just happened a few days ago, but I don't want to discuss it here."

"Yeah, I hear you, and I understand. I'm sure everything will come to light."

"It always does."

There was brief silence, and then I asked, "So, how's business?"

"Business is okay," he answered, "you know, things are steady. I'm not rich, but I'm able to maintain."

Words exchanged between us were kept to a bare minimum, and I didn't want to force it. Will didn't have much to say either, as he continued to touch up my hair in silence. He was done touching up my fade in about fifteen minutes, and I gave him forty dollars— twenty dollars for the cut and twenty for the tip.

"Thanks for the tip, Brock," he said.

I nodded and said, "You take care of yourself, Will."

"Wait; I'll walk you out."

We walked outside, and I turned around to face him and asked, "Do you believe that I've been a good friend to you?"

"What do you mean?" he asked.

"It's a straightforward and honest question, Will. I know I haven't been around much since I went away to college, and you might feel like I left you hanging or something."

"Yeah, man, you've been good to me. You gave me fifty grand to open up this shop, and you didn't even ask me to pay you back."

"Aside from the cash I gave you for the shop, do you feel like I went my own way? Come on, keep it real with me."

"Okay, all jokes aside, I felt a little envious of you when you went away to play college ball, and I felt snubbed by every college that offered me a scholarship but backed off once we went to jail that summer. Your dad pulled some strings for you to get in Union once the University of Illinois reneged on your scholarship, but I had to fend for myself once my mom died after graduation."

"I'm sorry about that, Will…"

"It's was like you weren't down for the hood anymore," he continued, "and you made it and didn't look back. I was angry at you for a long time, but then you gave me the money for the shop…"

"Just because I followed my dream to be in the NBA doesn't mean I stopped being your friend, Will. I'm sorry I didn't keep in touch with you more."

"I just thought you were like everyone else who made it—most people make their money and move on without giving anything back to the community. But you were different because you invested in me."

Will had a point—most people didn't give back. The majority of us got our fancy degrees and applied for jobs in corporate America because that was what we'd been taught, and most people didn't have to courage or wherewithal to start a business in the neighborhood.

"Yeah, the hood would be a whole lot different if we opened up our own businesses as a collective instead of getting jobs in corporate America," I said.

There was brief silence, and I finally said, "I gotta go, Will. Take it easy."

"Later, homie," he said, giving me a firm handshake.

I turned around and began to walk toward my car before he asked, "Hey, is the party for your sister Jasmine still on?"

"I don't know yet," I answered. "As far as I know, it's still on, but I gotta talk to Nikki about the details of it."

"Oh, okay. Is Malik still in town?"

"Yeah, he's still here."

"All right, let me know what's up."

"Okay."

I left the shop and headed to the car wash to get the stench out the interior. I then replayed my conversation with Will in my head. My gut tells me that he was the mastermind behind the whole scheme, and in so many words, he revealed his motivation for robbing me even though he didn't come clean about it. And I didn't expect him to admit his involvement, either. The goal was to find out if he had any animosity or jealousy toward me for going away to college without him, and I accomplished that.

However, why did he ask me if the party was still on, and why did he want to know if Malik was still in town? Were they planning to hit us again? I needed to know if Stanton was close to issuing any warrants to Will and his cohorts, and hopefully by the time I got home, my stepdad would have news for me. Now that I had reason to suspect that Will was behind the plot to extort money from me, the party for Jasmine would definitely have to be put on hold.

Meanwhile, I had to find something to do to occupy my time, because my date with Naomi was later on in the afternoon, and I wasn't going to head back home and back to Chicago for my date. I couldn't wait to see her, and I was looking forward to dinner and great conversation.

Chapter 20

Malik and Junior were watching the news at noon in the living room while eating McDonald's breakfast sandwiches. There was a shooting in the Gold Coast area the previous night, and a field reporter was interviewing a witness.

"Damn, we were just there Saturday night," Malik said. "Chicago is off the chain with all this gun violence…it happened across the street from the club that we were at."

"Yeah, this is crazy," Junior said. "I can't wait to get out of town and go away to school. If I stay here, something is bound to happen to me in these streets."

"A lot of your enemies are still around, huh?"

"Nah, most of them are dead or still locked up, believe it or not—but there's no code out here, and one of these punks is sure to try me. It's best if I start with a clean slate somewhere else."

"You can't speak that into existence, bro."

"I'm a realist, Malik."

"Do you think you'll come back after you graduate?"

"I don't know…maybe. I'm just focused on sticking to my plan and finishing school."

"And you will, BJ. I see your potential, and you'll be great at whatever you choose to do."

"Thanks, man."

Junior paused and asked, "Where's Brock?"

"He went to the city to get his haircut at Will's shop," Malik answered. "He was just leaving out when I woke up."

"Damn, I told him not to do that."

"Why not?"

"In case you haven't figured it out, Will is not to be trusted. He slept with Brock's girlfriend back in high school."

"Word? How come Brock is still friends with him?"

"I just told him about it last week…"

"You knew all this time and didn't tell him until last week?"

Frenemy

"I know it sounds messed up, but I was just a fourteen-year-old kid who didn't fully understand what was going on. I couldn't find the words to tell him that I saw Will and his ex-girlfriend Michelle kissing in the Walgreens parking lot."

"I'm sure he doesn't blame you, BJ."

"Nah, he wasn't mad at me—he was madder at himself for not recognizing what was happening in front of his eyes. Besides, I actually thought that they were already broken up, because they argued on the phone almost every day."

"What's done is done, I guess."

"Yeah, that's how Brock feels."

There was a noise on the front porch, and they heard a key turning the lock on the front door. Junior stood up and walked toward the door while Malik remained seated on the sofa. The door then opened, and Jasmine stepped inside first followed by Nicole.

"Hey, little sis," Junior said giving Jasmine a big hug and kiss on the cheek. "I missed you so much."

"I've missed you, too, BJ," Jasmine said. "It's been a long time."

"Yes, it has," Junior said. "Hello, Nikki."

"BJ," Nicole said as she nodded.

"Hello, ladies," Malik said.

"Hey, Malik," Nicole said, but Jasmine didn't say anything.

"Let me take your suitcase to your room, Jaz," Junior said.

"Okay, thanks," Jasmine said.

Malik swallowed the lump in his throat and walked toward Jasmine and asked, "Can I speak to you outside in private?"

"Sure, Malik," Jasmine answered.

They stepped outside, and Malik shut the door. The slight breeze blew Jasmine's hair in front of her eyes, and she took her hair and quickly tied it into a ponytail.

"I'm sorry if I made you feel some type of way last night," Malik said.

"I'm fine, Malik," she said. "I'm a big girl, and I can handle it. It's okay if you don't like me the way I like you."

Malik took her hand and pulled her toward him before he planted a kiss on her soft, sensual lips. She didn't resist him as their kiss became deeper and more passionate. He pulled away a minute later and gazed into her beautiful brown eyes before he asked, "Do you still think I don't like you?"

"What?" she asked, still shocked that he even kissed her.

"What I'm trying to say is that I'm really feelin' you, Jaz, and I think you're beautiful."

"I'm really feelin' you, too, but I couldn't gauge how you felt about me last night."

"I didn't want to come on too strong in front of your family—I wanted to remain respectful."

"I totally understand."

"Do you want to go out somewhere?"

"You want to go out with me?"

"Yes, pretty lady, I want to take you out right now."

"Okay, let me get settled in, and then we can go wherever you want."

"Great."

They walked back inside, and Nicole and Junior were arguing.

"I wish you'd get off my damn back, Nikki!" Junior shouted.

"You are not going to embarrass our family with your antics anymore, BJ," Nicole said. "You need to get it together."

"You are not my damn mother," Junior said. "I don't need a lecture from you or anybody else because I'm going to Union in the fall."

"How the hell is that possible? You dropped out of high school, remember?"

"Hey, hey," Malik interjected. "Calm down, you two."

"If you'd kept in touch with me like Brock and Jaz did, you'd know that I got my GED in prison," Junior said.

"I didn't know," Nicole said. "I'm sorry."

"And you should be proud of him," Jasmine added. "We all love you and want what's best for you, BJ."

"Yes, we do," Nicole said as she hugged Junior and kissed him on the cheek. "I love you."

"I love you, too, Sis," Junior said.

Chapter 21

Terrence was walking Spike through the neighborhood and ended up at the grocery store that was a few blocks from the apartment. He then clipped Spike's leash to the railing at the front entrance of the store.

"Sit, boy," Terrence said before he went inside.

He combed the aisles looking for some deodorant before going to a cooler to get some Miller High Life. He grabbed a twelve-pack of it and walked to the front to get in line. There was a woman with a big butt in front him, and he looked her up and down lustfully. She had an average-looking face at best, but an hourglass figure—the type of girl he was accustomed to dating. It was time to see if his game was rusty, so he placed his beer and deodorant on the counter and told the clerk he'd be right back. The woman had already checked out and was about to leave the store with her four grocery bags.

"Lemme carry your bags to your car for you," he said.

"Sure, that's very nice of you," she said.

"My name is Terrence, but my friends call me Terry," he said as they stopped in front of her car.

"Nice to meet you, Terry," she said, opening her trunk before he placed the bags inside. "I'm Tameka."

"Look, Tameka, I'm gonna cut to the chase. Do you have a man?"

"No, I just broke up with my boyfriend last month."

"Well, can I be your Mr. Goodbar?"

"That depends…"

"Depends on what, sexy?"

"Judging by your height, body type, and shoe size, if you got the weed and Alize, we can have a party."

"I'll tell you what: lemme program my number in your phone, and you can text me your address."

"Okay, I can do that."

She handed Terrence her phone, and he added his name and number to her contact list. He gave Tameka her phone back and said, "I'll slide through tonight, okay?"

"Okay, see you then," she said seductively.

Terrence went back in the store and asked the clerk if they had Alize, but he said they didn't have it. Terrence then paid for his beer and deodorant, and he unhooked Spike's leash and left the store. He observed the flashing lights when he turned the corner onto his block, and a DEA officer was taking Russell out of their apartment in handcuffs.

"What the hell is going on?" Terrence asked himself.

He stopped dead in his tracks and put his twelve-pack of Miller High Life on the ground before pulling his phone out his pocket to call Will while holding Spike's leash in the other hand.

"Sit, boy," he said before dialing Will's number.

"Come on, man, pick up."

Will's phone went straight to voicemail, and Terrence disconnected the call and dialed the shop's number.

"Hello," Terrence said. "Who's this?"

"Hey, Terry, this is Josh," he answered.

"Where's Will?"

"The cops picked him up early this afternoon."

"What for?"

"I don't know exactly—they were searching around for the stash but came up empty. Somebody must have dropped the dime on us, but luckily we didn't re-up yet."

"Damn, man, where did they take him?"

"He's probably at the county."

"Okay, later."

"Later."

Terrence picked up his beer, turned around, and began walking in the opposite direction. He had no money as the spoils of the robbery were still inside the apartment, and he couldn't retrieve his car because the DEA was in the process of impounding it. He walked aimlessly until he reached a vacant lot across the street from a Chase

Bank branch and cracked open a beer from his twelve-pack after leaning on what appeared to be a broken fence.

"Sit, Spike," he said.

He then pulled out his phone and dialed a friend's number.

"What's up, Deon?" Terrence asked.

"Nothing much, fam," Deon answered. "What's going on?"

"You wanna buy a dog?"

"Yeah, sure. What you got?"

"Spike, my dog…"

"How much you want for him?"

"He's a good dog—well-trained and a full-bred Rottweiler, you know—gimme $250 for him."

"How old is he?"

"He's six months old."

"You sure you wanna sell him?"

"Yeah, I gotta leave town asap."

"Done."

"Can you meet me in front of the Chase Bank on Eleventh and Roosevelt?"

"Yeah, gimme fifteen minutes, and I'll be there."

"Okay, see you then."

Chapter 22

Finding something to keep me busy until the early evening was a real challenge. I thought about catching a matinee, but nothing playing at the show piqued my curiosity. And there was the mall—Ford City, River Oaks, or Chicago Ridge malls—but I didn't feel like shopping, either. The Cubs were playing the Pirates at Wrigley Field, so I hung out at Chili's and sat at the bar until the game was over. I drank three cranberry juices and a Coke, but I didn't eat anything because I wanted to save my appetite for the seafood spot at Navy Pier. Thankfully, the crowd didn't pick up too much—I guess there were still a lot of people still at work—and I only had one autograph request.

The Cubs won 3-2 in ten innings, and the time was a couple of minutes past four. I tipped the bartender and left the restaurant. Naomi's apartment was nearby, and I still had a few minutes to spare. There was a floral shop in Lansing a mile or so away, so I bought her twelve long-stemmed roses and headed to her apartment. I dialed her number once I was in the parking lot of her apartment complex.

"Hey, Naomi, are you home yet?" I asked.

"No, baby, I'm just finishing up at work," she answered.

"Well, I'm waiting in the parking lot of your apartment complex. Do you need me to pick you up?"

"I'm sorry, Brock. Yes. I had to work later than I thought, and my car is back in the shop."

"What's wrong with it?"

"The alternator went out."

"I'm sorry to hear that."

"It's all right, I think it's time to buy a new car anyway."

"I'm gonna have to make that happen for you."

"That's so sweet, Brock…you'd do that for me?"

"Yes, I'd definitely do that for you. So, where can I pick you up?"

"I'm at the breakfast diner on Sibley and Paxton."

"Okay, I'll be there in a few minutes."

I disconnected the call and headed over there. Naomi was waiting for me outside where I arrived, and I pulled up at the entrance of the restaurant and got out the car to open the passenger side door for her.

"Thank you," she said. "Sorry I'm late."

"It's okay," I said, handing her the roses. "These are for you."

"Oh, thank you so much," she said before she kissed me on the cheek. "I love flowers, and these are beautiful."

"And so are you."

"Flattery will get you everywhere, young man."

"Do you want to go home and change?"

She paused and said, "I'm a little tired, and I have a final exam tomorrow morning. Can we just order a pizza and watch Netflix instead of going downtown?"

"Sure, we don't have to go out yet if you don't want to," I answered. "I just want to spend some time with you and get to know you better."

"I like the sound of that."

"Where do you want go for pizza?"

"Let's go to Beggar's. I'll call it in."

We headed to the Beggar's Pizza in Lansing after she called in our order, and there was a forty-five-minute wait. I parked across the street from the pizzeria and waited once we arrived.

"So, how have you been, Miss Hill?" I asked.

"Okay, I guess," she answered.

"What's wrong?"

"Family drama…"

"I can definitely relate to that."

"I saw my brother Nicholas' wife with another guy, and I don't know how to tell him."

"Just tell him the truth and let the chips fall where they may."

"Cecilia pretty much said the same thing."

"Yeah, how's she doing?"

"She had a little drama of her own, but she's doing fine."

"Let me guess. Man problems…"

"Yep, you got it. She ran into an old flame on Saturday, and things got a little heated…"

"Everything's okay, isn't it?"

"Yeah, all is forgiven. There was a huge misunderstanding between the two of them, but they patched everything up and are back together again."

"That's good to hear…I'm glad things worked out for the two of them."

She paused for a second and asked, "So, what drama do you have going on in your life? You looked a little out of sync when I saw you on Friday."

"Two thugs kidnapped my stepdad and demanded a million dollars from me," I answered. "I went through hell and back to come up with the money to free him."

"Oh my God! Is he all right?"

"Yes, I got him back without any complications, but the police are still looking for them as we speak."

"Damn, I'm so sorry, Brock. No wonder you were downing shot after shot last Friday."

"And I haven't even told my sisters about what happened yet—they just flew in town yesterday."

"I hope the police catch these degenerates—nobody's safe in these streets anymore."

Naomi sighed and asked, "Where did they kidnap your stepdad?"

"Can you believe in front of Chili's the day before I saw you?" I answered.

"Really?"

"Yes, my stepdad picked me up from the airport in Peotone, and they followed us to Chili's from there."

"How did they know you'd be at the airport last Thursday?"

"I believe my friend Will told them where I'd be…"

"Your friend Will betrayed you?"

"I'm afraid so."

"Unbelievable."

Naomi pulled out a hair tie from her purse and put her hair in a ponytail before asking, "So, what was the turning point in your life that brought you closer to God?"

"That's a good question, Naomi," I said. "I guess I realized that I needed to make the change in my life when I got busted for selling drugs the summer before my senior year in high school."

"You sold drugs?" she asked with a look of dismay. "I don't believe you, because you don't look like the type of guy who would've chosen the street life."

"Believe it, sweetheart. I was a totally different person back then—I was lost because my mother had just passed away, and my biological father was serving a life sentence for murder. I felt all alone because I detested my stepdad at the time, and I didn't care for stepbrother Brent Jr. or stepsister Nikki during that time period, either. I felt like my little sister Jasmine was all I had."

"How long were you in jail?"

"Sixty-one days, twelve hours, and forty-three minutes…"

"Damn, you remember your time spent down to the minute, huh?"

"I had nothing but time to think about the choices I made up to that point and prayed to God for forgiveness and vowed to give my life to Him if He got me out of my dismal situation."

"Well, I'm proud of you, Brock. You completely turned your life around by overcoming all of the obstacles placed in front of you, and you're very successful as a result of it."

"Thank you, Naomi."

"I just call it like I see it."

"What about you? What made you turn your life over to the Lord?"

"I realized that God was trying to get my attention after I broke up with Devon and had to drop out of school to get a job once my parents went through a divorce. I wasn't putting Him first in my life with the pre-marital sex, drinking, and smoking weed, either. I prayed to God for direction, and He showed me that I needed to change my ways and be a beacon of light for others."

"And people can see your light, Naomi. I know that I can see it."

"Thank you, Brock."

"I'm just calling it like I see it as well."

We continued to talk a few minutes more, and Naomi mostly told me about her day before I went inside to pay for the pizza while she waited for me in the car. I came back outside a few minutes later with the pizza and a half dozen cookies.

"I hope you want to eat a cookie or two for dessert," I said. "I don't eat them during the season, but I'm gonna splurge a little now that the season is over for us."

"I might try one," she said, "but I usually don't eat a lot of sweets. I try to watch my weight because I don't have time to go to the gym."

"I totally understand."

I put the car in drive and said, "I know you said that you can handle a long-distance relationship, but I don't want to put any pressure on you to make a commitment to me."

"What are you saying, Brock?" she asked in a disconcerted tone.

"I'm saying that you may not like me after our date tonight, and I don't want you to feel obligated to something that you may not want anymore," I answered.

"What makes you think that I wouldn't want you after tonight?"

"I've been burned numerous times by women in the past, and I don't want to get my hopes up."

"I'm sorry about what those other women did to you, but I'm not like that. Stop selling yourself short, Brock."

"You're right, Naomi. I'm sorry."

"You are a great catch, sweetheart, and if those other women were too blind to see it, that's their loss."

We arrived at Naomi's apartment fifteen minutes later, and I was taken aback when I saw her place. Her two-bedroom apartment was spacious, and the decor was impeccable.

"You have a very nice place, Naomi," I said.

"Thank you, Brock," she said. "Make yourself at home while I put these roses in water and freshen up a bit."

"Okay."

I turned on her television in the living room area while she took a shower. The news was on, so I decided to find out what was going on in Chicago that day. A stupid no-money-down car commercial blared through the television with a bunch of silly people dancing around like the auto dealership was giving away free government cheese or something to that effect.

Moments later, I received a text from my stepdad:

They got Will and Russell in custody right now. But Terrence is still at large. I told Nicole about the robbery and kidnapping.

I text my stepdad back:

Okay, great.

Naomi finished taking a shower and slipped into a fitted t-shirt and yoga pants. She looked at the pizza box on the stove and asked, "How come you're not eating yet?"

"I wanted to wait for you," I answered. "I can warm it up in the microwave."

"Thanks for waiting on me—I really don't like to eat alone."

"Technically, this is still a date even though we're slumming at your place."

"Eating without me could be viewed as being rude, but I feel so comfortable with you. I wouldn't have been offended if you did."

"I feel the same way. You look beautiful, by the way."

"Thank you, baby."

Her smile widened after my comment, and I picked up on her vibe that she wanted me to kiss her. I walked up to her and put my arms around her waist, and she placed her right hand on the back of my neck before I planted my lips on hers. Her cherry lip gloss tasted so sweet, and her lips felt so soft. The same spark that I felt in college was reignited as our kiss became deeper and more sensual.

We both pulled away from each other after a couple of minutes or so. I sensed that things were about to get too heated, and I believed she also sensed that we needed to put the brakes on the recreation of our unplanned rendezvous at the Quad toward the end of sophomore year at Union. We sat down on her living room sofa and faced each other afterwards.

"All I can say is wow," I said.

"I know, baby," she said.

"I don't know how I'm gonna continue to kiss you without wanting to make love to you, Naomi, but I can't and won't go against my principles."

"I totally agree, Brock. We have to contain ourselves, or else our many months of abstinence will be in vain."

"Let's just watch a movie, or we can sit and talk."

"We can talk some more, and then we can eat and watch a movie."

"Okay."

I sighed and said, "You're sexy without even trying to be, and it's taking every ounce of strength I have not to give into my flesh, Naomi."

"I want you every bit as much as you want me, but can we talk about something else?" she asked.

"Okay, my stepdad had just texted me and said the police have Will and one of the kidnappers in custody," I answered, agreeing with her that sex shouldn't be the topic of discussion, "and my stepdad told Nikki about what happened."

"That's great, Brock. The world is a better place with them in jail."

"Indeed it is."

"Do you have any other brothers or sisters?"

"Nope, just the ones that I told you about earlier."

"Nicholas is my only brother, and I don't have any sisters."

She paused and asked, "Does your brother know about what just happened?"

"Yes, he knows," I answered. "I shared the news with him the same day it happened."

"Your sisters are going to be pissed that they're the last to find out."

"I know, and I gotta brace myself for the fallout."

"So, tell me about your ex-fiancée and the reason why you all didn't get married," she asked, switching topics like the host of a daytime talk show.

"Megan Gonzales," I said. "I met her at the end of my first year in the NBA on a Southwest flight from Los Angeles. We exchanged numbers after the plane landed in St. Louis and were inseparable for the first five months of our relationship."

"Is she Hispanic?"

"Yes, she's Mexican and was born in Orange County."

"So, she comes from money, huh?"

"Yeah, you can say that. Her parents own two upscale restaurants…they have a location in Brentwood and one in downtown Los Angeles."

"Have you dated a lot of non-black women in the past?"

"No, Megan was the only non-black woman I've ever dated. I didn't see color with her."

"Why did you break up with her?"

"The first five months were great, but as we got close to our wedding date, she got cold feet and realized that she still had feelings for her ex. He's some dude that she has known since the second grade."

"You're the real-life Kelby character from the movie *Brown Sugar*, huh?"

"Yeah, I guess I am. I never thought about it like that."

Naomi paused and said, "I hope my questions aren't making you feel uncomfortable."

"Oh, not at all, baby," I said. "I feel totally safe with you."

"That's wonderful."

"So, why didn't you get married to your ex?" I asked, changing the subject.

"Kevin Sanders," she said. "It was simple—I didn't love him the way that a wife is supposed to love her husband. I got caught up in the fact that he asked me to marry him, and he was the only guy who ever proposed to me."

"You didn't want to hurt him, huh?"

"Absolutely not, because he was a great guy, but I couldn't spend the rest of my life living a lie. There was no spark, you know, like the one we have."

"We most definitely have a spark between us."

"I'm just happy that we finally found each other," she said, intertwining her hand with mine.

"So am I," I said.

"Are you ready to eat and watch a movie?"

"Sure."

Naomi picked a movie titled *Message From the King* staring Chadwick Boseman, and it turned out to be a good film despite the fact that most of the actors were unknown. We ate, laughed, and talked a little more while watching the movie, but we both fell asleep midway through it after snuggling up to each other.

I woke up first, and another movie had started playing already. I looked at my phone, and Nicole had sent me an angry text:

I've got a bone to pick with you, Brock! You could've at least told me what had happened to you and Dad!!

Naomi woke up moments later, and I said, "I have to go, baby. My sister Nikki is gonna read me the riot act when I get home."

"Are you sure you can't stay a little while longer?" she asked.

"I'm afraid not. We need to have an important family meeting regarding the fact that one of the kidnappers is still at large and could strike again at any given moment."

"Okay, I understand. I'm going to miss you."

"I'm going to miss you, too. I'll call you before I go to sleep tonight."

"All right. I probably need to go over some chapters one more time anyway."

"I'm sure it couldn't hurt."

I gave Naomi a warm embrace, and then we kissed just as passionately as we did hours ago. However, neither one of us pulled away from each other this time, and before I knew it, we were both half-naked on the living room sofa.

"I want you," she said as she continued to nipple and blow into my right ear while laying on top of me.

"I want you, too," I said as I removed her tube-top bra and unveiled her more-than-ample bosom.

I began to kiss her neck before she said, "Brock, wait..."

"What's wrong, baby?" I asked.

"We can't do this yet," she answered as she quickly put her bra back on.

"You don't want to?" I asked, still dizzy from the intoxicating scent of her shoulder-length, auburn-colored hair and cherry blossom shower gel.

"No, we can't."

I was glad she found the strength to bring our carnal desires to a screeching halt because I was ready and willing to give into temptation. I realized at that moment I was in love with Naomi because I didn't feel any shame or guilt about potentially going all the way with her.

"Damn, I know," I said. "We can't cross that line until we get married."

"What did you say?" she asked.

"You know, we have to find a way to contain ourselves when we're alone with each other," I answered.

"You want to marry me?"

"Yes, baby, I'd marry you tomorrow if I could. I've loved you since the first moment I saw you."

"Prove it..."

"Huh?"

"I said prove it, Brock. Marry me tomorrow."

"We can't get married tomorrow..."

"Why not?"

"Well for starters, we haven't even met each other's families, and I haven't bought you a ring yet."

"A ring is just a formality...I don't need a ring to remind me how much I love you or prove to me how much you love me."

"I'll tell you what, Naomi. We're supposed to be having a surprise graduation party for Jasmine on Friday, so you can invite your mom and brother. We will make our announcement to the family then..."

"You mean it?"

"Yes, baby, let me make an honest woman out of you. Will you marry me?"

"Yes, baby, yes! I will marry you!"

Chapter 23

Will had been sitting in an interrogation room for several hours after the police arrested him at his barbershop earlier in the afternoon, and they still hadn't allowed him to make a phone call after he was checked in at central booking. He was trying to figure out how the police tied him to any criminal activity because he hadn't re-upped his marijuana stash with Terrence and Russell yet.

Detective Stanton entered the interrogation room and sat across from Will. He said nothing at first and stared at Will, but Will didn't move or blink as he returned Stanton's stare with a blank expression of his own.

"I'm going to cut to the chase, Mr. Johnson," Stanton finally said. "You are being charged with first-degree kidnapping, which carries a minimum sentence of twenty-five years. Do you understand the charges being filed against you?"

"Lawyer," Will answered.

"Is that all you have to say?"

Will stared at him and said nothing. Stanton then got up from his seat and began to walk around the room.

"Let me paint a picture for you, Wilbur," Stanton said. "Your cohort Russell Martin is wanted for murder in Los Angeles, and he's being extradited back to the Golden State tomorrow morning. What this means exactly is that you and Mr. Martin will have separate trials, and according to him, you're the mastermind and ringleader of your little criminal enterprise…"

"That's not true! I had nothing to do with some damn kidnapping!"

"I beg to differ, Wilbur…we recovered approximately one million dollars from your house and Russell and Terrence's apartment collectively, and your cut was the same as theirs…"

"I want to cut a deal, cop. I'm not the ringleader, and the kidnapping wasn't my idea. I was backed into a corner and couldn't get out of it."

"You want to cut a deal? What's in it for us?"

"You say you have Russell in custody, but where's Terry?"

"He hasn't been apprehended yet. Why don't you tell me where he is?"

"Not without cutting me a deal. I can tell you where Terry is headed, but you gotta do something for me."

"You tell us where Chandler's headed, and I'll personally work something out with the DA because you agreed to play ball with us."

Will rubbed his chin and said, "He has a passport, and he's probably on his way to Detroit to cross the border at Windsor. We had it all planned out to leave the country after we hit Brock and Malik one more time."

"What's stopping him from doing the job by himself?" Stanton asked.

"We were supposed to work as a unit," Will answered, "and Terry won't deviate from Russell's plan. You might want to check out his girl Sherita Miller, though. He'll be stopping by there before he leaves town for good."

"Duly noted."

"And this whole kidnapping scheme was Russell's idea," Will continued. "He was the brains of the entire plan, and he needed Terry and me to pull it off."

"Why did you feel indebted to carry out this plan with Russell?"

"My cousin Rico was robbed and killed around this time last year, and he owed Russell a hundred grand worth of drugs and cash. I opened my barbershop shortly afterwards, and let's just say that he made me an offer I couldn't refuse..."

"So, you're paying off your cousin's debt by agreeing to sell Russell's drugs out of your shop?"

"Correct, sir."

"I see. So, why did you all target Brock Lane?"

"Brock and I went to high school together, and he's my best friend. Russell knew that Brock signed that big-time contract extension with the Wolves, and he wanted a piece of the pie. Russell also knew that I could find out when Brock was coming back to town so that he could come up with a plan to rob him."

"How does Chandler play into all of this?"

"He's just an accomplice like me, and I agreed to carry out Russell's plan so that my debt to him would be paid in full."

"And you'll be willing to testify all of this under oath?"

"Yes, sir."

"Okay. Your arraignment should take place no later than a few days from now, and I will talk to the DA sometime this week—depending on my schedule and his."

"Okay, detective."

Stanton then opened the door and said, "Guard, you can take Mr. Johnson back to his cell."

"What about my one phone call?" Will asked.

"And let this gentleman use the phone."

Chapter 24

Sherita heard a knock at her door, so she got out of bed to answer it. She sighed when she saw that it was Terrence through the peephole. It was an unseasonably cold forty-three degrees outside as the temperature had dramatically dropped, and Terrence didn't have a jacket.

"What do you want, Terry?" Sherita asked.

"I just wanna talk, Sherita," Terrence answered. "Let me in—it's cold out here."

"Go away!"

"Come on, Sherita! Give me five minutes of your time, and I'll be gone."

Sherita opened her door and said, "You have five minutes."

Terrence stepped inside her apartment and asked, "Have you seen my passport?"

"I don't know nothing about a damn passport," Sherita answered.

"Well, do you mind if I look for it? I think I left it on the top shelf of the closet."

"Yes, I do mind, but go ahead," Sherita said as she followed him to the bedroom.

Terrence began scanning the top shelf inside the closet and found his passport in a minute flat.

"It was right there where I left it," Terrence said. "Thank you."

"You're welcome," Sherita said, "now please, will you go?"

"You said five minutes...I need to know something."

"What?!"

Terrence pulled out his nine-millimeter pistol, pointed it at Sherita's head and said, "You snitched on me, didn't you?"

"I don't know what you're talking about, Terry," Sherita answered, her voice trembling.

"Don't lie to me...I can always tell when you're lying. I know for a fact that the cops traced my plate to your address, Sherita. I also know that you told the cops where Will's barbershop was located, and you told them that we were running drugs out of it."

"Don't hurt me, Terry, please...all I said was I haven't seen you in months, and I didn't know where you were. I swear I didn't tell the police anything."

"Okay, baby, I believe you, but I need some money to get outta town asap. Give me a grand from your stash to hold me over, and I'll let you live."

"I can't...I don't have any money to give you."

"You're lying to me again, Sherita! I'm gonna ask you one more time, or else I'm gonna blow your damn brains out."

"All right, please stop pointing that gun at me. My stash is in the guest room...follow me."

Terrence followed Sherita to the other room, and she opened a shoe box and pulled out a bundle of cash. She then counted ten hundred-dollar bills and handed them to Terrence.

"You always were a ride-or-die chick," Terrence said. "And I'm gonna need one more thing..."

"I'm not giving you nothing else, Terry..."

"Give me your damn car!"

"Hell, no..."

Boom, boom, boom! Terrence let off three shots—two to her chest and a fatal shot to her head.

He took the rest of Sherita's money and took her car keys off the kitchen counter where she always left them. He quickly trotted outside to her 2018 Dodge Challenger parked in front of the apartment and unlocked the door with the car key remote before starting the sporty vehicle with the start-stop ignition switch.

"I missed driving this whip," Terrence said to himself as he sped off the block.

Sherita had been a twenty-seven-year-old single woman with no kids who'd had a good job as an accounts payable clerk for the County. Unfortunately for her, she'd had horrible taste in men and made very poor decisions in life. Terrence and Sherita's tumultuous relationship had come to a violent end that night, and Terrence had had to alter his plans by entering Canada on the east coast instead of entering the country via Detroit because he sensed that either Will or Russell had told the police their escape route in order to save himself from life imprisonment. There was no honor among thieves, he thought.

Terrence was thirty miles or so into Indiana when he realized that he needed gas. He came off the Interstate at the Michigan City exit and stopped at a BP gas station a half mile from the highway. He parked in front of a pump and went inside, and there was only one other customer there. He got a twenty-two ounce of Budweiser because he wasn't able to finish the twelve-pack that he purchased earlier, because he'd ended up giving most of it away to Deon after he sold him his dog, Spike.

There was no one else in the store when Terrence approached the clerk's register. He then reached in his pocket and pulled out a fifty-dollar bill before placing his beer on the counter.

"Lemme get forty on pump two," Terrence said.

"No problem," the young man said.

"It's almost cold enough to snow, huh?"

"Yeah, it sure feels that way."

"Say, how much are those sweatshirts you got there?"

"Fifteen bucks."

"Here's an extra ten," Terrence said, handing the ten-dollar bill to the clerk. "Lemme get a black one in an extra-large."

"Can I get you anything else?" the clerk asked as he handed Terrence his change and the sweatshirt.

"Nah, I'm good. Thanks."

"No problem, man. Take care."

"Take care, fam."

Terrence proceeded to pump his gas after he cranked up his sound system a little bit. A Drake joint was playing on the radio as he put on his newly purchased, black sweatshirt. The sociopath who felt no remorse for killing his ex or the arrests of his two comrades drove off into the night after he filled up his tank. His phone rang, and he looked at the number and realized that it was Tameka from the grocery store calling him.

"Damn, I forgot about her," he said to himself. "I still wanna hit that."

He stopped at the red light that was a block from the Interstate and weighed his options. The light turned green after a minute or so, and he tossed his burner in the street before driving off.

CPSIA information can be obtained
at www.ICGtesting.com
Printed in the USA
BVHW030312270819
556902BV00016B/21/P